5/19/10

F

CHOPPY SOCKY BLUES

ED BRIANT

flux™
Woodbury, Minnesota

First Edition
First Printing, 2010

Cover design by Ellen Dahl
Cover image © redchopsticks/PunchStock

Flux, an imprint of Llewellyn Publications

Library of Congress Cataloging-in-Publication Data
Briant, Ed.
  Choppy socky blues / Ed Briant.—1st ed.
    p. cm.
  Summary: In the South of England, fourteen-year-old Jay resumes contact with his father, a movie stuntman and karate instructor, after two years of estrangement to impress a girl who turns out to be the girlfriend of Jay's former best friend.
  ISBN 978-0-7387-1897-2
  [1. Fathers and sons—Fiction. 2. Dating (Social customs)—Fiction. 3. Karate—Fiction. 4. England—Fiction.] I. Title.
  PZ7.B75883Cho 2010
  [Fic]—dc22
                                            2009030491

Flux
Llewellyn Publications
A Division of Llewellyn Worldwide, Ltd.
2143 Wooddale Drive, Dept. 978-0-7387-1897-2
Woodbury, MN 55125-2989, U.S.A.
www.fluxnow.com

Printed in the United States of America

ONE

My name is Jason Smallfield, I'm fourteen, and my father is an Imperial storm trooper.

He's right there, twenty yards away—on the opposite side of Trafalgar Street—all six foot four of him in his eighteen-piece battle armor and nifty blaster. As for me, I'm safely hidden in the deep early evening shadows of a crumbling archway. Safe for now at least.

You can tell it's him since he's not wearing his helmet, which is tucked under his arm. His thick black hair is swept back from his high forehead, and he's showing all his perfect teeth in a smile that makes it look like he's posing for a toothpaste commercial. In the movies they don't normally show you what storm troopers look like without their helmets, in case you start to think of them as real people. They don't want you to sympathize with them. But I think I'd have more sympathy for this particular storm trooper if his helmet was still on.

Of course he's been other things besides a storm trooper. In his time he's also been a henchman for SPECTER in a couple of James Bond movies; a cyberman in *Doctor Who*; and a zombie in *Shaun of the Dead*, not to mention a Viking, a Roman centurion, a pirate, a highwayman, and at one time, a not-very-realistic overgrown chimpanzee.

In other words, he's a stunt man. If you've spent any time at all in front of a screen that shows moving pictures, you've probably seen him. You know in *Return of the Jedi* when they attack the shield generator? My dad's the storm trooper who gets shot first and falls from the top of the bunker.

Even though he's been in other things, it's his storm trooper days he's most proud of. That's why he has the life-sized cardboard cutout of himself in the window of his very own karate dojo. And that's what I'm looking at right now.

True. He doesn't describe himself as a storm trooper on his business card. His card says: *Trevor Smallfield, defenestration is my vocation. Defenestration* literally means being thrown out of the window. It comes from the Latin word for window, which is *fenestra*. He had the cards printed after he was thrown out of his hundredth window, or so he says.

The word *defenestration* serves two purposes at the same time. It tells you what he does for a living, but using the word also makes him sound smart and intellectual, which he isn't.

Of course he doesn't just get thrown out of windows. He's also been lasered, blasted, thrown off spaceships, dropped off bridges, run over by lorries, and—on one occasion—he was even bitten in half by the Ravenous Bugblatter beast of Traal.

In the last few years my dad's been getting less work. This has nothing to with the fact that there's less evil in the world—I mean, how often do you see an out-of-work storm trooper? It has a lot to do with the fact that more and more stunts are done digitally rather than by real stunt men, and also quite a lot to do with the fact that at forty-five, my father's no longer quite so good at recovering from his defenestrations.

He first got into being a stunt man from being an expert at all things choppy-socky. He could do fight scenes. So now in his declining years he's returned to his roots. With an eye to the future, he opened one of the largest karate dojos in the South of England, at the top of Trafalgar Street, right in the center of Port Agnes.

Being kicked and punched by school children is far less damaging than being tossed out of high windows, and he can bring in no end of potential students by displaying the big cardboard cutout of himself in his storm-trooper's kit. I have to admit that it's not a bad plan. He can pass on a lifetime of physical injuries to a new generation, and at the same time keep making a living well into his dotage, because as time goes on, he knows that he's going to be less and less defenestrate-able.

So, that's my dad. He's a semi-retired stunt man who runs a karate school. Who could have a problem with that? I'm his son, and sons are supposed to look up to their dads—see them as role models—but I don't. I suppose I'd better explain why I've got it in for him. Lay it all out, as it were. The reason is that he's been a storm trooper for so long that he's lost touch with where the storm trooper ends and the dad is supposed to begin. It seems that you can always take the dad out of the battle armor, but you can't always take the storm trooper out of the dad.

You expect a storm trooper to be devious, unreliable, and untrustworthy, whereas you expect a dad to be honest, reliable, and loyal. My dad—on the other hand—is anything but honest, reliable, and loyal. He lied, he cheated, and he deserted his family. He's not just proud of having been a storm trooper, he still is one.

Why would I want to have somebody like that as a role model?

If anything he's an anti-role model.

I do not want to be like him. Does that make me a bad son? Maybe it does, but if I have to be a bad son to be a better person than he is, then that is the price I have to pay.

I'm going to go out of my way to be honest; I'm going to go out of my way to be fair; and if I ever get married—and I'm not sure that's likely given my looks and personality—but if I do, I will not walk out after twenty years just because I've found someone I like better.

When I say I'm going to *go out of my way* to be different, I mean it. I mean, I'm fighting genetics here, and in order to fight genetics I am going to have to go to extreme measures. This is not just one of those empty rants. I have even given up one of my favorite activities just to be different from him.

Namely karate.

I was always useless at sports. I threw like a girl and I couldn't catch. I was always on the losing side, and it wasn't just bad luck that I was always on the losing side. The team I was on always lost because they had me on their side and I was such a liability being so useless.

When I turned ten, Dad decided it was time for me to be initiated into the wonderful world of choppy-socky myself. Back then he didn't have his own dojo, so he gave me lessons at home in the back garden, just like he'd started doing two years earlier with my brother Hugh. At first I wasn't so keen, but after only a few weeks I could throw front kicks, back kicks, side kicks, roundhouse kicks, and even a presentable spinning hook kick. I still couldn't throw a ball, but I could throw a punch hard enough to splinter an inch-thick wooden board—at least with my left hand. After a month or so I wasn't just keen, I loved it so much I even slept in my uniform.

Dad was a qualified teacher, and I moved up through the belts, but then he moved out just before my blue-belt test and that was that. I could have gone to another dojo, but I didn't want to. Back then I couldn't really say why I didn't want to do karate anymore, but now I know. Even back then I sensed what I now know.

I think this is really the most important piece of my whole plan to be different than him. Choppy-socky was part of what made my dad what he is. Ever since he was ten he's lived, breathed, eaten, and drunk karate. When most people have a mental image of their dads, they probably see a kindly bloke mowing the lawn or cleaning the car. Whenever I have an image of my dad, I see him wearing his white *gi* and his black belt, crouched down in horse stance.

As far as I'm concerned he is choppy-socky, and choppy-socky is him.

I think if I can just resist the urge to do karate for the rest of my life, then everything else will just fall into place and maybe, just maybe, I will become a half-decent human being.

I'm so sure of this that I feel quite safe walking past his dojo in the evenings. I can even stand in the shadows like I'm doing now and watch him teach his teen class, which is the one I would be in if I was still training. I can watch the dozen or so blokes, and the odd girl or two, in their perfect white *gi* warming up with jumping jacks and push-ups. I can watch them practice their drills and forms. I can listen to the pops and slaps as they hit one another while sparring. I can do all that, and not have the smallest temptation to go in there.

Just to be on the safe side, I won't do *tae kwon do, judo, aikido, kung fu,* or *muay thai* either, because they all amount to the same thing in the end.

Never again will I throw a spinning hook kick.

If he wants to break bones, then maybe I will become a doctor and put them back together again. If I can't be a doctor I'll be an ambulance driver. If I can't be an ambulance driver I'll be a nurse.

That'll show him.

TWO

Jacqui Davidson's face is less than a foot away from mine.

I've never been this close to a girl, and I have no idea what will happen if I try to kiss her.

I suppose under normal circumstances there would really only be one way to find out.

She has eyes the color of oak leaves with the sun behind them, her mouth is open a fraction, and I can see a flash of her incisors peeping out from below her upper lip. Her teeth are far whiter than mine would ever be, even if I embarked on a program of perpetual brushing until I was fifteen.

Who would have thought that homework could get this interesting?

Not me.

I'd love to know what she's thinking about, because I suppose all things being equal Jacqui's actually Hugh's girl. On the other hand, I don't think Hugh has been giving her a lot of attention lately, so I think it's okay for me to be here with her.

If Hugh was still interested in her, then that would be a whole other story. I want nothing to do with breaking up relationships. I'll leave that kind of thing to my dad.

Right now Jacqui's looking straight at me, but she has one of those halfway expressions. I can't tell if she's about to break into a grin, or if she's about to look very serious indeed. I can't even tell if she's looking at me or through me.

It's probably her karate training. The thousand-yard stare.

I know I should probably just relax and enjoy being with her, but in addition to not knowing what she's thinking, there are one or two other things that bother me.

To begin with, she's far too fit-looking for me. She stays in shape by practicing kempo karate and vegetarianism.

I'm five foot four with gingery hair and—now that I don't do karate anymore—a pot belly.

I point out to Jacqui that I'm the only one in my family who looks like me. Hugh, my big brother, is tall and slim with straight dark hair, just like both our parents, and I have to give Jacqui credit as my orangutan-like appearance doesn't seem to faze her at all.

Even though Jacqui's a freshman art student from Palo Alto in California, which would make her eighteen or nineteen, the age difference doesn't seem to faze her any more than my absence of matinee-idol features. And why should it? This is the modern world after all.

I'm certainly not complaining. I'm more than happy

to be an item with an older woman if she looks like Jacqui Davidson.

The physics, the chemistry, and even the biology aren't a problem, but I'm not so sure about the geography. How far can this thing go when we live oceans apart? Would she be prepared to leave Palo Alto, which looks pretty nice in the photos, and move in with me in the rainy seaside town of Port Agnes-on-Sea in the south of England?

I'm not keen on the fact that she does karate either. I mean, if we got serious she might tempt me back into a dojo.

But then who am I to talk? Nobody's perfect, least of all me, so I'm not going to ask perfection of Jacqui.

Ah, what the heck? I'm always being told that I think too much, that I'm my own worst enemy, and that I should just relax and go with the flow. I don't know what will happen when I try to kiss her, but I do know that I have a time limit.

I lean towards Jacqui a centimeter at a time, like a cat stalking a sparrow. She only has to move an inch, and my mouth will brush the empty space between us.

I take a final glance at the ocean in the background, on either side of her dark, shiny hair. The rolling surf reminds me of the tuna sandwich I had for tea. Blast. I didn't brush my teeth, but with her mouth about three inches from mine, it's probably not the best moment to run off to the bathroom.

I pass the point of no return, tilt my head a little to the side, and take her upper lip between both of my lips. A butterfly kiss. A little nervous. Unthreatening.

I press my lips together. It's so realistic I almost expect her eyelids to flutter down, but they can't because, of course, she's only a photo.

But she does move.

She sort of crumples actually, and there's a nasty tearing sound.

The glossy paper of the magazine sticks to my upper lip. I pull back.

My lower lip stings as a tiny flap of skin comes off.

I taste salty blood.

Blast and bugger.

There's now a small, white triangular tear right across Jacqui's mouth.

My little fantasy is torn to shreds.

What makes matters worse is that Jacqui Davidson is in one of Hugh's *Girls on Parade* magazines. I look at the date on the cover.

Blast! It's this month's. I should have known. Why did I think that just because it was hidden a long way down in his stack of comics—and it was sort of battered-looking—that it was an old one? I can't throw it away. It's probably one of the first things he'll look for when he comes in, and if it's missing he'll know exactly what happened to it. I can't put it back either. He'll have a fit when he sees the torn page. I suppose I could glue the little flap back down and hope he doesn't notice that two of the nudie pages are stuck together.

No. He'd never notice a thing like that. Not really.

No two conscious thoughts connect in my mind as I shove the magazine into my waistband, throw my jacket on, race downstairs, and out the front door. Next thing I know, I'm barreling down London Road on my bike, and it's only when my knees start to hurt that I come to my senses. The reason my knees hurt is that I keep banging them on the handlebars. The reason I bang them on the handlebars is because I haven't ridden the bike since I was twelve, and I haven't ridden the bike because Dad bought it for me. Two minutes with a spanner and I could have at least raised the saddle and made it rideable.

Then I get this hollow feeling. *The cables!* I squeeze the back brake, and the rear wheel slides on the asphalt. One of them seems to work at any rate.

I turn left into the leafy tunnel of Adelaide Road without even realizing why, then I notice the big trash can at the corner of Springwell Crescent. I freewheel over to it, prop the bike at the curb, and look all around. Nobody. There never is.

I pull the *Girls on Parade* out of my waistband and hold it over the garbage can, but I can't resist one last look.

I lick my finger and try to stick the torn flap of paper back down onto Jacqui's lip, but it just keeps popping back up. Her mouth is ruined. Even if I squint my eyes I can still see the tear.

I've destroyed the thing I love.

Is there someone I'm related to who destroys love?

I rather think there is.

I let the magazine slip through my fingers and it slumps down into the pile of Coke cans, banana skins, and soggy newspapers.

I'm back on the bike and heading west along Marine Drive when it hits me that my ability to act without thinking is probably a hangover from my karate training.

I have to nip that in the bud, but only when I'm finished with what I have to do in the next twenty minutes.

I turn up Little Preston Street, then lock the bike to a meter outside Palma's Newsagents. I can't lock it to the meter right outside Palma's because there's a biggish-looking dog attached to that one, so I give him a couple of meters leeway as I don't know how long his lead is. The dog gives me a sidelong look as if he knows exactly why I'm here, and he doesn't approve. I try to ignore him as I cross the pavement and push in through the door.

"What'cha, Jay," Gary Palma looks up from his perch behind the counter. "How's Hugh doing?"

"We thought he had The Black Death last week," I say. I turn my back on Gary and scan the magazine racks. "Unfortunately it was only a cold, and he got better."

Girls on Parade is right there. All I need to do is reach up to the "Over Eighteen Only" rack, pull out the copy from behind the plastic screen, buy it, and be on my way. The reason I don't is that there's another customer. In a perfect world I could buy the magazine with absolutely nobody else around, but I suppose Gary has to be there, seeing as he's one of the few newsagents in Port Ages-on-Sea who sells porn to underage youths. On the other hand, he must have watched this process so many times that he's immune to it. He's probably a bit like a doctor in that respect. The big problem is not that there's another customer, but that she is a girl—she's wearing a dark red sweater, which I think is the Cardinal Newman uniform—and what makes it worse is that she's about my age.

I don't have forever, but Gary isn't going to let her stay and read the entire magazine, so she'll have to leave eventually. Meanwhile I have to bide my time, so I slide a copy of *Metal Detecting in Focus* out of its slot and flip through it.

"The Black Death can be nasty," says Gary. I glance over my shoulder. He's looking down at his book again. "They shove a foot-long syringe up your bum."

"No. I think that's rabies." *Metal Detecting in Focus* is even less interesting than you might think from the title, so I slide it back into its space on the shelf. I'm actually starting to get impatient. Why doesn't the girl leave? Is Gary just going to let her stand here and read a whole magazine? Maybe I could just reach up and grab *Girls on Parade* without her noticing. She looks fairly ensconced in her magazine, so she might not notice. What's more, she's wearing the kind of thick-rimmed glasses that librarians wear in soap operas, so she might not even see what I'm up to even if she does notice.

Come to think of it, she is holding the magazine about two inches away from her nose. Maybe I ought to chance it, because even if she finishes up and leaves, another customer might come in, and I'd have to wait all over again. I begin to crawl my hand up the shelves past the lower magazines.

"Yeah," says Gary. "That's the National Health for you. There's probably a waiting list to be thrown in the ditch an' all."

Just as I'm about to reach for the *Girls on Parade*, the girl customer says, "That's not right at all."

I almost have a heart attack. My hand freezes on its path towards the top shelf. I can't believe it. Not only did she see me reaching up for a porno mag, she's actually telling me off. Even though she's already seen me, I lower my hand a bit to make it look as though I wasn't really reaching for the forbidden magazines on the top shelf, but for something more acceptable on the shelf below. After a minute I look around at her, and she says, "They don't shove the foot-long syringe up your bum; they put in your stomach."

She brushes a loose strand of brown hair off the lens of her glasses, and then the oddest thing happens. A little dimple appears in each of her, admittedly, slightly chubby cheeks, she gives me a quick smile for about a half second, then looks serious, then smiles again. It's a bit like someone tossing a coin to see what expression to wear.

I have no idea what to do. I'm standing about two feet away from this girl who is—and I have to point this out—quite pretty. I don't know what to say. I'm standing like I'm playing statues with my hand hovering in front of *Good Housekeeping*, and it doesn't help that the girl is looking at me like she doesn't seem to know if it's okay for her to smile at me or not. I don't know anything at all about girls. All my life I've been at all-boys schools. I don't have a sister. I haven't spoken to a girl since I was in nursery school, and that was Vida Sarstedt who only spoke to me to say, *So there!* after she bit me. I clear my head and tell myself that based on what this girl has said, it doesn't seem like she was commenting on whether I could buy a porno mag or not, so maybe she didn't see after all.

With that I let out a long breath, and I look around at Gary. He should know about girls; after all, he's been selling both *Good Housekeeping* and porn since he was in short trousers. Something has to have rubbed off on him over the years. But he's no help. He's gone back to reading whatever it was he was reading under the counter, and I can't say anything to attract his attention as I still can't talk.

Then I make the fatal mistake of glancing at her again. I think I was hoping that she'd have gone back to reading her magazine, but she's still staring at me, and my eyes are locked onto hers. They're just lovely. They're brown and shiny, and almost as big as the rims of her glasses. Then she does that quick half-second smile again.

If I don't breathe in, I'm probably going to fall over. If only I could tear my eyes away from hers I would be able to breathe in, and if I could breathe in I think I would be able to speak. Mustering every ounce of strength, I tip my head forward and look down.

The first thing I notice is that she's not thin, but then she's not fat either. Then I realize that I'm now staring at her boobs, which are actually quite big. Even though I don't know a lot about girls, I know I'm not supposed to do that, so I force my eyes back up to her face again.

The thing that gets me is that she is just lovely. Even with the glasses. She might even be prettier than Jacqui Davidson. What's more, I don't think Jacqui Davidson would use a word like *bum*, and I like that this girl said it, because it means that she's not too stuck-up.

She opens out the magazine to turn the page. I suppose

she's got fed up with waiting for me to say anything back, but then I notice the cover of the magazine—*Black Belt Monthly*.

Without even thinking, I say, "I do karate," then immediately put a hand over my mouth.

I'm just about to correct myself, and tell her what I meant to say was that I used to do it, when she looks up from her magazine and gives me a huge grin.

"What rank are you?" She has nice teeth as well.

"Green belt," I say. Once again without even thinking.

"Really?" she says, and she smiles even wider if that's possible.

"Yeah," I say, and I want to say more, but I think I've exhausted this particular subject.

She folds her arms over her boobs, with the magazine in between. She crosses one leg in front of the other and leans on the magazine rack. Then she uncrosses her arms, brushes a strand of hair behind her ear, and says, "Yeah. Me too."

"Yes. No," I say. I point at the magazine. "I sort of guessed that." I do this silly laugh, *hah hah*, then I stop and actually say, "The magazine. You know." In case she thinks I'm pointing at her boobs.

"Oh yeah." She unfolds her arms, looks at the magazine, and does a sort of double take as if she didn't know it was there. The she does this deep laugh, *ho-ho-ho*. "Be a funny choice of magazine for me to read if I didn't do karate, know what I mean?"

Then she does her laugh again. Her voice is really nice. It's a little deeper than I expected with her being a bit short. I then realize I'm laughing too.

"Yeah," I say. "It would be like reading, I dunno…" I scan the magazine rack. "…be like reading *Seventeen* if you were twelve."

"Right," she says. "Or like reading *Women's Realm* if you're a brick layer."

"Or like reading *Good Housekeeping*"—my brain whirls—"if you live in a shed."

Ho-ho-ho. "Or like reading *Fishing Times* if you're actually a fish."

"Can fish read?"

Ho-ho-ho. "They can read quite well, but they can't turn the pages with their little fins."

I'm about to make one more of the magazine jokes when she says, "Actually, I meant I'm a green belt as well." Then she folds her lips over her teeth, nods, and says, "Mmm."

"It's the best belt to be," I say.

"Right," she says. "It really is." She shuts the magazine, smooths it out, and props it back on the shelf next to *The Ring*. "Apart from the next belt up."

"Oh yeah. The blue belt."

"I always wanted to be a blue belt. I really like blue. Mmm. Especially blue eyes." When she says that, the weirdest thing happens. She folds her lips over her teeth and she goes bright red. "I suppose I should be going." She steps away from the shelves and as she does, *Black Belt Monthly* clatters to the ground. Right away she crouches down, but I drop to my knees and get there first.

I grab the magazine and hand it to her. I want to tell her that I prefer brown eyes, but all I get to say is, "Aye—"

She says, "Wah…" and then, "You first."

I say, "No. You first."

We stand up together. She flattens out the magazine, and puts it back. "I was going to ask you which dojo you trained at."

"Total Karate." Now it's my turn to go red. "It's in Trafalgar Street." *Oh no. What am I saying?*

She opens her mouth into an "O" shape.

"It's my dad's dojo. He runs it." At least that part is true.

The "O" shape gets bigger.

"He's one of the highest-ranking black belts in the country."

"Wow," she says, and then a dog starts barking outside. It's a deep bark. *Oof oof oof.* She closes her mouth and looks past me to the door. "I really do have to go," she says.

I don't want her to go. A deep sadness wells up inside me. If only I could keep her here for another minute. I rack my brain for something to say. "Where do you train?"

"All-Fitness Karate. It's in Portland Road, just past Boundary Road."

"I think I know it."

The dog barks again. "Oh, Rosko."

When she says this, I somehow know that the big, disapproving dog I saw outside is the one that is barking, and is also hers.

She moves past me to the door, and my sadness comes back, but she only opens the door a fraction then turns to me and asks, "Do you like dogs?"

18

I hate dogs. I'm terrified of them. Especially big ones. "Yes," I say.

"Do you want to come and say hi to Rosko?"

"Okay."

The moment she's outside, the dog leaps up, tugs on his lead, and wags the entire back half of his body.

The girl crosses the pavement, then squats down and wraps her arms around his head. "You bad, bad puppy."

The dog looks at me as if to say, *I don't really like this, but she does it all the time and you get used to it.*

The girl unwraps his lead from the meter and grins at me. "Do you want to pet him?"

I swallow and lower my hand to the top of his head for a moment. He doesn't even bite me.

"It must be amazing to have a dad who does karate." Her voice sounds different outside. Not so deep. She does her laugh, *ho-ho-ho.* "I can't imagine my dad doing karate. He'd probably say his job takes up too much time."

"Well, I suppose karate is my dad's job," I say. "Actually, it's both his jobs. He's a stunt man as well."

"A stunt man!" Her eyes get wider than her glasses. "Does that mean he jumps off skyscrapers?"

"Well, he doesn't really. He just makes it look like he does."

"Still, it sounds like a lot of fun. You are so lucky. That must be really amazing."

"I don't know." I shrug. "He's just my dad."

"Well, okay," she says. Rosko tugs on his lead. "I suppose I'd better be going."

"Okay." The sadness is almost unbearable, but I don't know what else to say.

She lets Rosko drag her a couple of paces then she turns. "I don't know if this sounds a bit weird, but I'm actually having my blue-belt test." She brushes her hair back. "I mean, it's not for three weeks, but you could come along and join in. I don't know how you do sparring at your place, but at All-Fitness Karate it's usually all light, and low contact, but when they do the testing the sparring is full contact. It's brilliant. You can hit the black belts as hard as you like. I mean, you pick up a few bruises, but you really get to find out how good you are. I bet you'd love it. Go on, say you'll come."

"Yes," I say, and the sadness disappears. "Me too. It sounds brilliant. I mean, I'm testing for my blue belt as well, and you could come to my test, too."

"Okay. It's a deal. We can support each other even if we're at different dojos."

She lets the dog drag her backwards a few feet and then an idea hits me so hard that I almost want to slap my forehead. "By the way, what's your name?"

"Tinga."

"T-I-N-G-A?"

"Yeah. Kind of a goofy name, but it's the only one I have. What's yours?"

"No. I like Tinga. I'm Jay."

"It's nice to meet you, Jay."

"Me likewise," I say, which I don't think makes any grammatical sense.

She lets herself be dragged to the end of the block, then she waves and vanishes from sight behind a truck.

I can't move from my spot. I'm in absolute shock. I don't know anything about this kind of business, but I actually think I have a girlfriend, or at least a potential girlfriend.

Then, in the same way that the adrenaline drains out after a sparring session, the shock fades and reality rushes in to fill the empty space. The first thing I notice is that my face hurts from smiling. Then the realization hits me. What have I done? I haven't trained for two years. I've sworn never to train again as long as I live, and now I've not only told her I'm an active green belt, but that I'm about to move up to a blue belt.

Then I do this zoning out thing again. Next thing I know I'm walking beside the bike—because I'm fed up with banging my knees on the handle bars—pushing it up Walton Crescent. It's just as well I'm almost home because I think I want to just go and hide under the bed forever.

I've blown everything.

It's not just that nobody wants to be friends with a liar. I don't want to be a liar. I'll leave that sort of thing to Dad.

I must be completely mad. Why did I have to tell her I was still doing karate? She probably would have liked me even if I wasn't still practicing. But now I've told her I'm a green-belt-going-on-blue-belt, I'm going to have to live up to it somehow.

I could show up at All-Fitness Karate and make out like it was all a big joke. That would really impress her.

I could just walk away and never see her again. I mean,

it's not so bad. Maybe in another four or five years I'll get another chance to have a girlfriend.

I could just show up in my *gi* and my green belt, but I would get beaten to a pulp sparring. I'd probably die of a heart attack I'm so out of shape. Then they'd all stand around the bloody mess on the floor—which would be me—and say, "Well, he shouldn't have lied about being a practicing green belt."

I suppose I could start training again, and make my lie into the truth. Sort of backwards honesty. Trouble is, I would have to train like a fanatic every single day between now and June 4th, and even then I would still take a beating.

The last plan is actually not bad. The big drawback is that there are only two dojos in Port Agnes. The one I can't go to. And the other one I can't go to. I mean, I can't exactly show up at Tinga's dojo, because that would be kind of stupid. Equally, I can't go to Total Karate in Trafalgar Street, because it would mean training with Dad.

Maybe I should just go without doing any training, get mangled, and be exposed as a liar. That would be a lesson to me I wouldn't forget next time. Next time I met a girl, I'd have a big sign up inside my head: DO NOT LIE!

Things could not be worse.

Just as I'm thinking that, a motorbike pops and crackles past me. Hugh's Kawasaki. I've been all the way over to Palma's and I've forgotten to get *Girls on Parade*.

Bugger and blast!

THREE

"And he's turning into such a good-looking young man," proclaims *Mother!* as if she's revealing the punch line of a joke. "I saw him cycling down Eastern Road just last week." Her voice drifts into the kitchen from where she's having a conversation, out of sight, on the hall phone.

She always drops her voice when she wants to talk about me and I'm in the next room, so the *he* in this statement probably isn't me. It's okay. I know I'm not good-looking, and I've come to terms with that. What could possibly make me think that Tinga would be interested in me? Even if I could make up for two years of no training in just three weeks, all she did was invite me to her blue-belt test. Anyway, she probably just wants me to come along because I look out of shape, and she's going to have to spar with all of the upper belts and I look like I'd be a pushover.

I wish I could just stop thinking. I need a distraction. I put down my slice of toast, reach across the kitchen table for the *Daily Telegraph,* and try to tune out the conversation in my head.

Perhaps this is a good place to talk about *Mother!* When I reached the age of ten, the Parent-Formerly-Known-as-Mummy decreed that Mummy was babyish, and she would henceforth be rebranded as *Mother!* In addition, she decreed that the word *Mother!* be pronounced while standing upright with the shoulders thrown back, enunciated fully and correctly.

Especially the final *r.*

I haven't quite got the hang of the pronunciation yet, and the name tends to materialize as *Muerthuergh!* Something like a Parisian onion seller cursing and then clearing his throat.

The end result is that the woman who brought me into the world, whom I'm quite fond of, remains in my mind as Mummy. I try to avoid using any form of address whatsoever when talking to her in person, but for the purpose of telling this story I will persevere with calling her *Mother!*

"Don't be silly," says *Mother!* "You know perfectly well where he gets his looks from."

Meanwhile, back in the kitchen, the headline on page two of the *Daily Telegraph* reads: *Another Scorcher! It's The Hottest May For Twenty Years.* This is hardly news, as my sweaty forearms are already stuck to the table.

Under the headline is a picture of *pretty Melanie Arkwright* in one of the Trafalgar Square fountains. She has dark hair and a big smile. Just for half a second I think the photo is of Tinga, and an electric shock runs through me. I look at the way Melanie's boobs stretch out her white T-shirt to try to stop myself thinking about Tinga, but it makes it even worse.

It's no good. I can't get her out of my head. I'm either going to have to chop my own head off or start training again.

I feel better now that I've made the decision, but only for a second. A second after I make the decision, there's a little voice in my head that asks me how I know she actually fancies me. How do I know she doesn't just want to be a friend? How do I know that after torturing myself for an hour a day, every day, for the next twenty days—then getting beaten up on the twenty-first day—she will actually want to be my girlfriend? I mean, everything I know about girls comes from Hugh's porno mags, and I have a feeling they're not the most reliable source of information on the subject.

There has to be someone I can get advice from, but who?

Maybe this is one of those occasions when a dad might come in handy, but I point-blank refuse to approach the only dad who's available to me.

If I was desperate enough to need his advice, then I would probably be too desperate to have a potential girlfriend.

"I know, Mildred," says *Mother!* "It would be such a shame, but I really do think it's just a phase they all go through."

Mildred!

Mother! must be talking to Mildred Briscoe. She can't know more than one Mildred. Most people don't know any Mildreds at all.

A few years ago, we spent just about every Sunday with the Briscoes. Half the time they would come to us, and the other half we went to them. Then all in the space of one day, we just stopped seeing them. For some reason I think it had something to do with their son, Malcolm. I wanted to ask him about it at school, but when I got there on Monday he was gone, too. It's funny. Malcolm and I were best mates for years, but then we drifted apart. He started to get very touchy about things.

Wait a minute. Cogs begin turning in my head. I have an idea.

"That would be lovely, Mildred," says *Mother!* "I'll see you in about half an hour."

Uh oh. *Mother!* is about to finish. I still have Melanie Arkwright's boobs spread out in front of me. I don't want her to come in and see me looking at them. I'm about to turn the page when a small headline catches my eye: *Boy, 14, In Coma After Karate Kick.*

It's only a single paragraph. Maybe I have time to read it.

"Jason, sit up straight, and take your elbows off the table. You look like a lout."

"Sorry." *No!* How did she get from the hall to the kitchen doorway in one second? Too late to read the karate piece, and too late to turn the page. I slide my plate over Melanie Arkwright's picture with my elbow.

Jewelry clatters and stiletto heels click on the linoleum. "After I have my coffee, I'm just going to pop over to Ikea for a couple of hours," says *Mother!* She has a cigarette packet, a pair of sunglasses, a lighter, and the car keys all clutched in one hand. Maybe the two-inch-long nails help. "I'll leave you to hold down the fort."

"Oh. Okay."

She squeezes behind my chair, wafting perfume over me, and with one hand slides the jar of Nescafé out of the cabinet above the stove.

I have to word this exactly right. I probably have one chance, and one chance only, to get this right.

I turn around in my seat to face her. "Was that Mildred Briscoe?"

"Do you listen to all my conversations?" She throws the cigarette packet, sunglasses, lighter, and car keys onto the counter.

"Um. No."

"Your father used to do that." She unscrews the plastic lid of the coffee jar and throws it down next to the other stuff. *Fantastic.* Yet another wonderful way in which I'm just like Dad.

"If I'd listened to my mother's phone conversations, I'd have been given castor oil and sent straight to bed." She hurls a teaspoon of coffee powder into her cup, then unplugs the kettle and takes it over to the sink.

I give thanks that my maternal grandparents now live in New Zealand, where their child-rearing techniques have probably been incorporated into Maori tribal initiation ceremonies.

"Yes. For your information, that was Mildred Briscoe." She fills the kettle from the cold tap, then plugs it in.

"I thought Dad said we couldn't have anything to do with them anymore."

She squeezes back behind me and I look down to make sure Melanie Arkwright's boobs are still hidden.

"I don't know if it slipped your notice"—she squeezes back behind me, hauls open the fridge door, then stares inside as if she's got something in there she's been saving for just this moment to throw at me—"but your father hasn't actually been around recently to enforce his precepts."

"It was all to do with Malcolm, wasn't it?"

She pulls out a carton of milk then wags it at me. "Jay! You have to learn to stay out of what doesn't concern you."

"But it was because he took up karate and he didn't go to Dad's school, wasn't it?"

Mother! pulls the sad face that people make when they're trying not to smile.

"No." She shakes her head. "It was more complicated than that." She shakes the milk carton to see how much is in there, then opens the top and smells it.

"Do you know if he still does karate?"

Now she smiles, but she doesn't look at me. Instead she looks out of the kitchen window, which is—by some coincidence—the direction of the Briscoes' house. "I actually don't know, but he is in extremely good shape." Now she looks at me.

Yes. I get it. Malcolm is in good shape as opposed to another person right here in this room that isn't.

"I wouldn't be a bit surprised if he was still training," she says.

"And he goes to All-Fitness Karate?" I ask.

"What are you getting at, Jay? I can tell when you're up to something."

For half a second I actually consider spilling the whole story to her. But no more than half a second.

Okay. Here goes.

"If you can be friends with Mildred ..." I rotate my teacup clockwise. Slowly. I tip back the last cold mouthful. "... then why can't I be friends with Malcolm?"

"I thought you didn't like him," she says. She starts to head back to the kettle, then stops. "Wait." She turns again and heads to the door. "Let me call her back."

Mother! click-clicks back out to the hall with the milk carton.

A moment later I hear, "Oh. Mildred. I wanted to ask you something."

Now her voice drops down to a whisper, and my ears burn.

I crane my head to one side to see if I can make out the words that are hidden in the mumble. Then I hear, "You don't have to do that, Mildred. That's very sweet of you." She drops her voice to just above a whisper again. "I'll go and ask him. He's just got in from school and he's having his tea."

This time the *he* is me, and sure enough, the click-click of the imperial stilettos returns towards the kitchen with the sort of briskness that implies that they bear time-sensitive information.

"Mildred's invited you to go over and have a swim in

their pool," announces *Mother!* She pulls a cigarette out of the pack by the kettle, then fires it up with the little gold lighter. She glances at my bulging stomach. "I don't think a swim would do you any harm."

"And Malcolm's going to be there?"

"Yes."

And that's it. Simple. I've just made a decision.

If Malcolm trains at All-Fitness Karate, then he has to know Tinga. If he knows her, then at least I can just ask him about her. Maybe. Just maybe I could find out something about her from him.

FOUR

I chain my bike to the chestnut tree in front of Castle Briscoe and push through the creaky iron gate.

As I make my way across the front garden to the porch, I think about all of the times I used to play here over the years. I have plenty of time to do this. It's not the world's biggest front garden, but on the other hand I wouldn't be surprised to see elk grazing in the middle distance.

Something bothers me. I used to love coming here. Malcolm had amazing toys that were always better than mine. He had the swing set when we were little, and then the swimming pool later on, but what I really loved coming for was the *Playboy* magazines.

Most dads keep motoring or fishing magazines by their bed. Malcom's dad keeps *Playboy* next to his bed. Right out in the open. A big stack, as big as Hugh's stack of comics—well, okay—Hugh's stack of comics *and* porno mags. I mean, does Mr. Briscoe lie in bed in the evenings and read

Playboy while his wife flicks through the knitting patterns in *Women's Realm*? It seems a little odd. But then on the other hand, I have to admit that Mr. and Mrs. Briscoe are still together, unlike some married couples I could name.

Mother! seemed to think I didn't like Malcolm. Maybe I didn't. Was I only friends with him so I could go over to his house and look at the *Playboy*s? Obviously I'm not interested in looking at *Playboy* anymore, now that I have a girlfriend—at least in theory. I suppose if somebody held a gun to my head and forced me to look at a *Playboy*, it wouldn't be the end of the world.

On the other hand, I'm still coming over here for an ulterior motive, which is that I want to pump Malcolm for information about Tinga.

I've been on the other side of this equation, and it's not a very pleasant place to be. I used to have a ton of friends who wanted to come over to play at my house, but they didn't want to come over because they liked me. Most of my friends were only friends because they wanted something from me. They wanted to see my dad. They knew what he did—because Hugh had told them—and they probably thought they'd see him doing things like mowing the lawn, putting up shelves, and cleaning the car in his Imperial storm-trooper kit. They probably thought he'd let them play with his laser blaster out in the back garden. What they actually saw, if my dad was home, was a bloke sitting on the sofa reading the *Daily Telegraph*, wearing a cardigan and—more often than not—a neck brace.

So when I went to my new school, which Hugh doesn't

go to, I just told everyone my dad had a shop. That way people would only want to come to my house to see me.

I've been at that school for three years and not a single friend has come back to my house.

I've always thought it had something to do with our house. Maybe it's just too ordinary.

On the other hand, Malcolm's house looks almost exactly like Henry VIII's castle—apart from the double garage. It even has a turret, which is where Malcolm's room used to be. According to *Mother!*, Mr. Briscoe had the house put up by his own builder so it can't be that old, but I always wished we could live in a house with battlements and windows that look like you could fire arrows from them. I bound up the steps to the porch, which has some trellis-work and—in keeping with the Henry VIII look—plenty of space for chopping heads off.

I pull the bell chord. Chimes sound from far inside, followed by a braying bark. I'm not making this up; they really do have a bell cord. Halting footsteps shuffle on the other side of the door. A latch is unfastened, and the door creaks open to reveal—not a burly knight with a poleaxe—a girl of about Hugh's age, with hair so blonde I actually have to shield my eyes from the glare.

"Yes. Hello. What do you want?" She has an interesting accent. I can't recall any of the Briscoes having interesting accents, so she must be an au pair or something. She's about a foot taller than me, with rosy cheeks and curiously small green eyes. She's probably pretty, but her face is fixed into a kind of a permanent-looking scowl.

"Yeeeeoww!"

This sound is so inhuman that I think for a second it's going to be Flossie the dog.

I'm several feet up the trellis-work when I realize that it's actually Malcolm whooping as he slides down the hardwood floor in his socks. At least it's a carbon-based life form with Malcolm's head attached to it. He looks exactly the way I remember him, with his mouthful of grinning teeth and ears that look like they've been positioned for satellite reception. His body is another story. Last time I saw Malcolm, I was bigger than he was. Now he almost has to bend down to fit through the door.

Anyway, he knocks the au pair out of the doorway, onto the stoop, and onto her hands and knees on the porch.

"Malcolm, you horrid boy," she says, which puts it in a nutshell.

"Oops, sorry, sorry, sorry, Siggur." He reaches down to help her up, but she ignores his hand. "I'm sorry, Siggur. It was an accident. I couldn't stop." He steps over her, then slaps me on the back. "What'cha Jay, me old mate, me old china, me old pal. This is Siggur. She's a language student." He leans close to my ear and says, "She's going to be bloody impossible for the rest of the day now." Then in a louder voice, "She's from Denmark, you know," in much the same tone he might have used to tell me she practices naval gunnery in her spare time. "You know about Scandinavians, right?" He leans even closer and elbows me in the side. "They eat cheese for breakfast."

"They do?" I really can't think of anything else to say.

Malcolm shakes his head. "That was supposed to be a joke?"

"Oh, right. I get it." Yeah. Malcolm. Now I remember.

I jump down from the trellis-work and offer Siggur my hand. I really do want to help her up, but the helping-hand position also gives me the opportunity to see down the front of her T-shirt. I force myself not to look though. I don't need to do that kind of thing anymore, now that I have a theoretical girlfriend.

On the other hand, what harm can one quick glance do?

She ignores my hand anyway, turns her back on me, and walks back into the house dusting herself off. I suppose I'd have a permanent scowl if I was a language student at the Briscoes. We follow her into the cool, shadowy hall. I catch sight of Malcolm's double. He appears to be standing next to an apelike creature, at least a foot shorter than him. My arms tingle with disgust as I realize I'm looking in the hall mirror at Malcolm's and my reflection. True. He is older than me, but only by about a year. Not really enough to explain the size difference. Now it looks like he should be Hugh's friend rather than mine.

I turn to face Malcolm and now he has his hand out to me. "Long time, no see," he says. The silly grin has gone from his face and he looks almost sad. "It's been a dog's age. How's tricks, and all that stuff?"

"Not too bad." I take his hand and we shake, but then I try to pull my hand back and he doesn't let go. Instead he stares at me for a second, then he looks down at my chest, my stomach, my groin, my knees. All the way down to my feet, then all the way back up again. Is this some new karate thing? Is he trying to figure out how much difficulty I'd give him in a fight?

Finally he gives me my hand back and says, "Let's get changed and go for a dip." Then he turns and heads up the staircase which is almost wide enough for two cars to pass each other.

I follow him up a couple of steps. With his back turned, and me just behind him, it seems like a perfect time to broach the subject that's dear to my heart. "Are you still doing karate?"

He stops and turns so fast that I bump into him. "What do you mean, *Am I still doing karate?*"

"Nothing." I take as step back down. "I just meant are you still doing it?"

"Oh, sorry. I thought you were being sarcy. *Hup-hup. Hey!*" he yells. He leaps up to the little landing where the stairs turn, shouts "*Kee-yah*," and swings into his stance.

I want to tell him a simple *yes* or *no* would have been enough, but I lose my balance and have to grab hold of the banisters to stop myself from tumbling back down to the hallway.

"Funny you should ask," he says. "Come and look at this."

He runs up the rest of the old, familiar staircase three stairs at a time, slides across the broad landing, and stops in the doorway to his room.

"Look."

Right in the middle of the room, hanging from some

kind of gubbins on the ceiling, is a blood-red punch bag with *Londsdale* stamped across it in big yellow letters.

"My old man put this up last week so I can train for my brown-belt test. Watch." Malcolm leads me in, takes a small pair of boxing gloves from his bedside table, and slides his hands into them.

"*Kee-yah!*" he shouts. He jumps into a low stance with his feet spread wide, then shuffles towards the bag.

Pop-pop-bang! He punches and kicks the bag, then slips to one side. *Bang-bang-bang.* He throws a series of rapid roundhouse kicks. A machine-gun kick. He keeps moving around the bag, throwing a flurry of punches and kicks, then he does some jump back kicks. At one point his foot whirls so close to my face I can almost smell cheese.

I've got to admit that he looks good. I wouldn't want to tangle with him. In fact, I wouldn't want to be on the receiving end of one of his kicks, not even by accident, so I slide my feet back till they hit the bed, then I let myself tumble back onto the quilt. Out of danger, I have a chance to scan his books and posters, along with the bitter smell rising from under the blankets.

Above the headboard is a row of LITTLE BUDDHA comics, and above them is a two-foot-tall poster of Bruce Lee's *Fists of Fury*. I have nothing against Bruce Lee personally, but he was Dad's ultimate hero, so I don't watch any of his films anymore.

Some of my earliest memories are of sitting on Dad's lap on the sofa and watching videos of *Fists of Fury* and *Enter The Dragon*. I had no idea why all these people kept hitting each other and screaming, but I loved the way Dad shouted back at the telly.

Malcolm slows, returns to the middle of the room, drops his arms to his sides, and yells, "*Kee-yah!*"

He catches his breath and says, "What do you reckon?"

"Malcolm," I say. "You are a machine! No doubt about it."

"*A machine?* You think I'm too mechanical?"

"No. *No.* I mean you have power, energy." I wave my hands in the air. "Stamina. You just keep going."

"But not a lot of skill."

"No. I mean, yes. You have tons of skill."

"Do you really think so?"

"Yes!"

"Oh. Thanks," he says. "I mean, I think I'm getting there. Slowly working out the kinks. I have to have it ready for my test in three weeks. I have my white, yellow, orange, green, blue, and red belts. Once I have the brown, I'm one away from my black belt. Here, this is the special thing I've been working on."

He crouches into his stance again, but this time he backs away from the bag.

I'm nowhere near him, but I have no idea what's going to happen so I slide across his bed and flatten myself against the wall.

"*Kee-yah!*"

He leaps so high he just misses the ceiling. In midair, he spins his hips into a crescent kick that just slaps the bag.

Then, without touching the ground, he throws a back kick, and then a spinning hook kick.

Bang! The last kick bends the bag almost double and sounds as loud as a gun shot.

"Whoa!" I say.

"Yeah." *Puff.* "Right," he says between breaths. "Tornado." *Puff.* "Kick."

"Looks really good."

He screws up his face. "It's got to be more than just good-looking. It has to *be* good."

I put my head in my hands. "I'm telling you, mate. I wouldn't want to be on the other end of that," I say. Now that he's resting, I feel safe enough to move up to a sitting position on the edge of the bed.

"Really?" He looks disappointed.

What can I say? I think this is going to be a long afternoon.

"Really," I say.

"Oh," he says. "I was hoping you could give me some pointers."

"Me?" I want to tell him that ugly as it is, I'm actually attached to my head for sentimental reasons and would like to keep it somewhere near my shoulders. I have a vision of my head flying out of Malcolm's bedroom window like an old football.

"Well. Yes." He eases off the gloves. "You're a black belt. Right?" He puts the gloves under his arms and tucks his shirt back in. "You were a green belt two years ago, so I just assumed you must be a black belt by now."

"I had to take a break from training." I think I need to change the subject. I need to get to the point. "You train at All-Fitness Karate, right?"

"Right," he says slowly. "What about it?" I swear he gets into a kind of loose fighting stance.

"I know somebody who trains there, and I wanted to ask you about her."

"Oh. Now it all makes sense." He gives me a sidelong look. "I don't see you for two years and then you just show up out of the blue. Obviously you want something."

Oh, man! "Look. It doesn't matter. Let's just have a swim."

"No. Really, I didn't mean to snap at you. Tell me."

"Okay."

I'm just about to tell him when Siggur's voice reverberates through the floor from downstairs. "Boys! If you don't swim now you'll run out of time!"

"Come on," Malcolm throws the gloves back on the table and hauls his trunks out of a drawer underneath. "We ought to get changed if you want a dip in the pool. It's nearly five and I've got to walk Doggie-doos before supper."

"Alright." I want to talk about it here and now. I want to tell him it's important, but I suppose I'm his guest so I pick up my towel and head for the door.

"Wait," says Malcolm. "Where are you going?"

"I'm going to change in the bathroom."

"What's wrong with changing in here?"

"Er. Nothing." Well, nothing and everything. I hover for a second out on the landing.

"Anyway, we sort of keep the bathroom free as a female changing room."

Even though I don't like exposing myself, I don't like looking coy either, so I go back into his room. He shuts the door behind me, which is understandable if Siggur is around, but then he locks it, which isn't encouraging.

"I just want to get through this test." He pulls off his shirt and throws it on the bed. "They say the *sensei* doesn't test you unless she knows you're going to pass. They say nobody ever fails, but I have a bad feeling about it." He kicks off his socks. "And there's always a first time. Right?"

"Seriously Malcolm. From what I've just seen, you have nothing to worry about." I squat down and untie my shoelaces. "Anyway, this other person I know—"

"Oh yeah." He unbuckles his belt and lets his jeans slide to the floor.

I really don't want to see this. I shuffle around so I'm facing away from him. "Yeah. She's a girl," I say to the punch bag that I'm now facing. I can't really talk to him without looking at him. I turn my head so I can just see him out of the corner of my eye, but as soon as I do, I see his black underwear fly towards his bed and land on his shirt.

"Really. What's her name?" He turns towards me, butt naked, with his hands on his hips staring at me. "Are you going out with her?"

"Well. Sort of." I pretend to look at something on his ceiling. In actual fact, I can't tell him anything. "Well, I don't know." Is he standing like that just by chance? Or is he doing it to show off? I can only see his penis out of the corner of my eye, but it fills the corner entirely, like a World War II barrage balloon. I shut my eyes tight, and then at that precise moment the doorbell chimes and makes me jump about a foot off the ground.

Downstairs, Flossie erupts into snarls and barks like a grumbling old lady. Another dog answers with a deeper bark from outside.

"Huh?" Malcolm frowns, shuffles over to the window, then smiles at whoever is down there.

I open my eyes. He has his trunks on. I heave a sigh of relief.

"Hiya!" He waves, then turns to me. "It's my girlfriend," he says. "I can't believe I forgot she was coming over."

What! Don't tell me he has a girlfriend! I suppose it makes sense though. Better toys, better dad, better at karate. I bet he's already seen her with nothing on. On the other hand, I suppose it's starting to look like he really is about the best person I could have gone to for advice. I wonder where he met her.

As if he can read my mind he says, "I met her at the dojo."

Jealousy side kicks me in the ribs, but I brush it away, hop over to the window, and stand next to him. By the time I get there, all I can see is the porch roof, but as the first wave of jealousy fades I start to take a long-term view. Compared to me, he's an expert on this kind of thing if he has a girlfriend. I can talk to him man-to-man.

"Flossie! Put a sock in it!" he yells as he strides over to the bedroom door. "Come on, Jay. Hurry up and finish changing."

He stands in the doorway, staring at me.

"Go and answer the door." I unbuckle my belt as slowly as I can. "I'll come down when I'm ready."

"It's okay," he says. "I'll wait for you." And he just stays there, staring at me.

I turn my back on him again and try to break the world land-speed record. I take off my trousers and pants at the same time, but one foot gets stuck in the trousers, the other gets caught in the pants, and I end up dancing around the room on one leg as I try to put on my swimming trunks.

I do keep my shirt on though. I know it's pathetic, but I can't bear to expose my pudgy upper-half to the world. Especially if the world includes some probably gorgeous female who's used to drooling over Malcolm's tanned and buff torso.

I follow Malcolm down the stairs, and a few moments later our bare feet slap on the floorboards as we cross the hallway. Flossie is jumping up at the front door, spinning in circles, and making yelping noises. Malcolm takes hold of the dog's collar with one hand while he unlatches the door with the other. I stand partly behind him as he pulls it open. The moment an inch-wide crack appears, a dark snout pushes through from the outside. Flossie's claws slide and scrape on the floorboards.

The dark snout is connected to a hairy head.

I'm not an expert on dogs, but this one has a very familiar look.

My body begins to shut down. A numbness crawls up my legs, and by the time Malcolm's girlfriend is all the way through the door, I can't even move my little finger. I want to swallow, but I can't close my mouth. What's worse is that even though I can't close my mouth, I can't breathe. I literally have to gulp the air in to stop myself from falling over.

"Hi, Tinga." Malcolm's voice drifts over to me from a galaxy far away. "This is my friend, Jay."

And there she is. Standing rigid in front of me. If anything, her eyes are even bigger than her glasses today. I wish she'd close her mouth though.

I feel like I've turned into a wooden robot. A door creaks open in my chest and something heart-shaped tumbles out. It rolls across the floor, bounces down the porch steps, and plops into the fish pond, where it sinks straight to the bottom.

"Jay." Malcolm's voice makes me jump. Something bad just happened and I can't think what it was. *Oh yeah*. I remember now. All my hopes, dreams, wishes, longings, yearnings, desires, and needs are lying in the stinky mud at the bottom of the Briscoes' fish pond.

Apart from that, everything seems okay.

"Jay," says Malcolm. "Meet Tinga." As he says it, Flossie jerks him out onto the porch, and for a moment he can't see either me or Tinga.

I shrug and force a grin, which is more of a grimace.

She smiles back, waves her index finger in front of her mouth, then does a shush gesture by holding the finger upright in front of her lips.

I do a sad-face nod. Tinga winks, and gives me a thumbs-up. I'm not totally sure why she doesn't want me to tell Malcolm we already know each other, but I would jump off the roof wearing my underpants on my head if she asked me.

FIVE

Siggur is swimming breaststroke laps in strict accordance with the Olympic rules for the stroke, which means she keeps her head above the surface at all times so her hair doesn't get wet.

Tinga is changing in the bathroom.

Malcolm tests the water by standing on the edge and dangling his toes in. This seems like the kind of thing Granny Smallfield might do, but having seen Malcolm naked, I don't think he'll ever need to feel insecure about his manliness.

Dipping your toes in the water seems pointless to me. The water's going to feel icy when you first get in, and comfortable after about five seconds unless it's (a) boiling hot, which it isn't otherwise there'd be steam coming off the surface, or (b) below freezing, which it can't be otherwise there'd be a layer of ice across the surface with sea lions poking their snouts through circular holes to breathe.

Unlike Malcolm, I run at the pool as fast I can, then

hurl myself off the side. I absorb the icy shock, keep my eyes open, and brush the bottom of the pool with my stomach. Maybe the ten-ton weight in my chest will stop me from coming back to the surface. So I suppose that's the end of that. Just as I was beginning to hope the impossible might come to pass. I have to look on the bright side, and there is one. Two days ago I was well on my way to becoming a completely different person to Dad, but since yesterday I've lied about the fact that I'm still training, I've been devious in becoming friends with Malcolm again for my own purposes, and I've been preparing to take up karate again. Now I don't need to do any of that.

I've lost the girl but I've kept my principles. Seems like I'm doing the right thing. I don't have to worry about her blue-belt test anymore. There's no point in even going now. I have the feeling that I could just stay down here forever. No Dad. No karate. No Tinga—or at least no lack of Tinga. I have plenty of air in my lungs. I almost feel as if I could fall asleep in my blue universe. I crawl along the tiles until the dark blue wall appears; then I let myself float upwards.

I break through the surface and wipe my eyes just in time to see Siggur climbing out. I can't take my eyes off her backside. I'm fascinated by the way it stretches out her emerald green suit. She turns at the top of the ladder and makes eye contact. I look away quickly, but not quick enough. I feel myself go red, even in the water. Nevertheless, I look again as soon as her back is turned.

Before I can get a good look, Malcom's hand pushes me back under. I see him scramble up the ladder as I get my bearings. I shake the water out of my hair and follow, but as soon as I get to the top Siggur yells, "Boys. No horseplay."

I turn around to say *Sorry*, and as soon as my back is turned, some Malcolm-type force hurls me back into the water. I leap out to take revenge, but before I get the chance a strange dark-haired girl tiptoes down the steps from the back door, then jogs across the grass towards the pool.

It takes half a second to recognize her, and once again I lose the power of movement. Being able to move is definitely something I won't take for granted in the future.

She's wearing the kind of blue one-piece suit that girls on swimming teams wear, and has her arms folded across her chest as if it's cold. She stops right between us. "*Brrr*," she says, and dances from one foot to the other. "I hate this bit."

"Oh. It's not too bad." Malcolm's voice startles me as if I've been asleep for a few months. "Just lower yourself in slowly."

Then she tilts her face up to look at me.

Yes. She tilts her face up to *me*.

She frowns as if she's seen me somewhere before—which she has, only she was wearing her glasses at the time.

I flex my jaw to see if it works. It does. I'm rooted to the spot, but I won't have to speak like a bad ventriloquist. "I would just take a running jump. Get it over with in a second," I say. At least I think it's me that says it. The voice coming out of my mouth is not one I recognize. It's the voice of someone much older and wiser than me. The voice of somebody who once knew happiness many years ago, and will not know it again, but life must go on. The pain is still there, but it's more like a memory of pain now. An old friend who has been at my side on the rugged pathways of life.

"I think I like the idea of the running jump."

Me too. I like the idea of Tinga preferring my idea. I do. I really do.

She takes a few paces back.

I still can't move my feet, so I have to twist at my hips in order to keep looking at her.

She unfolds her arms and swings them a couple of times as if she's forgotten she had them, then she charges straight between us towards the pool. The way she's waving her arms, I expect her to make a huge splash, but she organizes herself into a missile midair and makes an almost perfect entry. A moment later she pokes her head up, swishes her brown hair around, and spits out a stream of water.

"Call that a dive?" says Malcolm. "Watch this." He jogs to the springboard, takes three steps, produces a forward flip, and enters the water with about as much splash as you might expect from tossing in a coin.

This leads to a diving contest between Malcolm and Tinga. The best thing I can do is a cannonball, but nobody seems impressed. Nevertheless I keep jumping in, because I do have one neat trick. I can vault straight out of the pool without using the ladder. I suppose in the back of my mind, I want Siggur to see me and be impressed. After all, Tinga's out of the picture now, so I'm a free agent again. Not that I ever wasn't, or so it now seems.

It's a lost cause. Siggur's lying back on the lounger reading a paperback, by someone called Knut Hamsun, through a pair of sunglasses with frames the size of portable televisions. Plus, the sunglasses are so dark that I'm not sure she can even see the book, let alone me.

Eventually I just plant my arse on the edge of the pool, dangle my feet in the water, and wonder what my next disappointment will be.

Just as I'm thinking it's the end of the world, a pair of wet feet splat next to me, a wet arm brushes against mine, and Tinga plants herself beside me.

"*Brrr,*" she says again, only this time she really is cold.

I have an almost uncontrollable urge to put my arm around her. Just to warm her up.

"Fancy meeting you here." She folds her arms and rubs her shoulders with her hands.

Where do I begin? "How?" I say, which I suppose is a good beginning for a question. I'm just not too sure what the next word is going to be. I look around for inspiration.

Siggur glances at her watch, gets up from the lounger, and goes back into the house.

Malcolm finds some goggles. He snaps them onto his face, slips into the water, and swings his arms into a crawl.

He has the look of someone who's about to try to beat their personal best for a set number of laps, which is good, as it will give Tinga and me a few moments of privacy.

"How well can you see without your glasses?"

She glances from side to side. "Who said that?" *Ho-ho-ho.*

"No, really."

"Really. I'm very short-sighted." She gets up on her

hands and knees and puts her face about a foot away from me. "I can see you pretty well from here."

I'm so surprised that—even though I don't want to—I shuffle away from her.

"Sorry," she says. "I know I look a bit scary, but I just wanted to see you in focus."

"No. *No*," I say. I shuffle closer to her again. "It's the opposite. I think I'm the scary-looking one." Then as quick as I can—so she can't respond—I say, "Why don't you want Malcolm to know we saw each other?"

"Well. To be brutally honest." She gives me a pained look. "I really like Malcolm, and all that, but he can be a bit weird."

Weird? Some images I don't want to see half-form themselves in my head.

I must have looked shocked because then she says, "Oh, no. Nothing like that." She sits back down next to me and sits cross-legged. "When I'm here, he ignores me." She nods at the pool. Malcolm is now doing the backstroke. "But he likes to know where I am and what I'm doing."

The half-formed images of Malcolm's weirdness seem intent on fully forming themselves.

"Don't look so worried," she says. She puts her hand on my shoulder. The warmth spreads down my arm. "It's okay. Listen, I want to know more about your dad being a stunt man. That's something I'd really like to do."

She swivels around to face me with her back to the pool.

"Do you know how girls can get to be stunt men?"

"Well…" I say.

"Or stunt women, I suppose."

We both get splashed with cold water as Malcolm starts working on his butterfly.

"Actually, there aren't many women who want to do it. In most of the dangerous stunts where they need a woman, it's actually a bloke dressed as a woman."

"Really." She looks so disappointed that I wish I hadn't said anything. "But not always?"

"No. Not always."

She grins at me. "Did your dad ever dress up as a woman?"

"No." Something inside me snaps. I can't help rolling backwards onto the grass. In a heartbeat all the tension, all the worry, all the sadness drains out of me, and I splutter with laughter. "He's too big. *Splutter.* Wouldn't look right. *Splutter.*" Finally I manage to get my laugh under control, although I can't sit up. "There are actually blokes who specialize in women's stunts."

"So how did your old man get into it?"

I push myself back into a sitting position. "He did karate, then he got offered a job on a James Bond film. *The Man With The Golden Gun.* It's a really early one with Roger Moore, but it's packed with great martial arts."

"Then one thing led to another."

"Exactly," I say. "You've seen *The Man With The Golden Gun*, right?"

"No." She gives me a big grin and shrugs her shoulders

up to her ears as if she's apologizing for the fact. She's so enthusiastic that I half suspect she's winding me up. But she's for real. "My mum and dad don't really like me watching that kind of film."

I wonder what *that* kind of film would be, but I don't wonder out loud because I don't know her that well and don't feel like prying.

Then she says, "Do you like Bruce Lee? He's my absolute hero." She does her shoulders up to the ears thing, but this time her eyes actually get wider than the frames of her glasses.

Now I'm really confused.

I'm confused because her parents won't let her watch James Bond, but will let her watch Bruce Lee. It seems to be splitting hairs. I mean, Bruce Lee has been referred to as the Chinese James Bond.

But I'm more confused because my own personal rules—which I'm willing to admit are a little crazed—will permit me to watch James Bond, but not Bruce Lee, on account of dad being a big Bruce Lee fan.

The most confusing thing of all is that I'm just totally happy to be confused. In this happy little conversation, I've forgotten that my whole world had fallen apart. Although thinking that reminds me of the reality of the situation, but before I can sink into a total gloom, she says, "Which is your favorite Bruce Lee film?"

"*Fists of Fury*," I say, because it was the poster on Malcolm's wall.

"Mine too," she says. She beams at me. It's like I'm on a dark road caught in a set of car headlights.

"I thought your favorite was *Enter The Dragon*." Malcolm's voice drifts up from the pool where he's swimming the breaststroke.

Wow. He can hear us talking. How much has he heard?

"Not anymore," says Tinga. "The best bit is the *nunchuk* fight. It's like Bruce Lee turns into some kind of animal, and it's really him. No special effects or anything. Everyone thinks of Bruce Lee as an action figure, but he was a really amazing actor." She looks from Malcolm back to me. "Plus he had a sexy bod to boot."

She leans closer to me. I know she wants to tell me something without Malcolm hearing, and she must have had the same thought about him being able to hear us while he's swimming.

"I didn't want to say anything because I think we're just about to break up." Then she folds her lips over her teeth. "I don't want to get you involved in it." She shrugs. "I mean the break up. It could get messy."

My heart is a fist hammering on the back of my sternum. *If they're going to break up…* but wait. This is sad. I shouldn't be happy.

"That's awful, Tinga." I didn't have to say her name, but I wanted to. "What makes you think it's going to end?"

She glances at the pool and I follow her eyes, but Malcolm is still underwater. He has quite a set of lungs.

"I walk Rosko in Wish Park every day at four." She licks her lips and leans even closer. "Malcolm used to come to the park every day to meet me with Flossie." She takes another look at the pool. "Now he maybe comes once a week."

"Maybe he's nervous about the test or something."

She holds her finger up to her lips.

"Anyway, the one day I didn't go to the park turned out to be the one day he came to the park to see me."

"Oh." I blow out a long breath.

"That was yesterday, when I went to the newsagent."

"I see."

"It might look a bit weird if I didn't see him, and I did see—" She doesn't get a chance to finish what she was saying.

"Oh, man!" Malcolm flops down right between us, breathing hard. "I really feel like I'm getting the hang of the breaststroke."

Now I feel awful. I wish I hadn't talked about him behind his back. I feel dadlike again, but a part of me doesn't feel so bad.

"I have to get back for supper," Tinga says, "otherwise I'll be crucified."

"Aren't you going to come to the park?" says Malcolm. He's lying on his back.

"No. I really do have to go," says Tinga. She stands up. "I'm going to get dressed." She takes a few steps towards the door. "I'll see you."

Malcolm still doesn't get up.

She's leaving. Aren't they going to kiss or something?

Maybe it's me. I'm making them feel awkward. I stand up and throw myself back into the pool again to give them some privacy. As soon as I'm in the water my curiosity gets the better of me, so I push myself away from the side on my back, so I can keep my eye on them. Malcolm's still on the grass, but Tinga gives me a smile. Maybe it isn't for me. Maybe it's for Siggur. I glance over at the lounger, then I remember she went back inside.

"It was nice to meet you," says Tinga.

"Likewise."

"We'll have to talk more about Bruce Lee sometime," she says. "Maybe I'll see you down here again. Or maybe in Wish Park. I usually walk Rosko at about four. After school."

"Yeah. I'd like that." That's funny. She just told me that. Maybe she forgot.

She takes her towel and heads back into the house.

Once she's out of sight, I vault out of the pool, then crash out on the grass next to Malcolm. "She's gorgeous, you lucky beggar."

"Yeah," he says. A little uncertainly. Flossie comes over. He reaches up and slaps her back. I wonder if he understands which *she* I'm talking about. Maybe he thinks I'm talking about Siggur.

"Tinga," I say. "She's really nice."

"She's alright," he says, which seems a little inadequate.

"Her parents sound a little odd if they won't let her watch James Bond."

Malcolm nods. "Yeah. Her dad's like a lay preacher. That's sort of like an assistant priest. She's not actually allowed to have a boyfriend. That's why we meet with the dogs, because the only way she's allowed out on her own is if she pretends she's going to walk the dog."

"Wow. That sounds almost barbaric," I say. "I mean, I'm

supposedly a Catholic, but nobody ever tries to pull anything like that on me."

"I'm not even that into her really. I've been wanting to split up with her, but I keep putting it off." He looks at me as if he wants me to agree, but I don't so I just nod. "I don't know why. I mean, I know she's a lovely person and all that, but she's just not my type. My dad doesn't like her much either." He grins at me. "He calls her the chub-nugget."

I have to admit that I have mixed feelings about Mr. Briscoe. I like that he not only has *Playboy* all over the house, and doesn't mind who reads them—or more to the point—looks at the pictures.

But I don't like that he bad mouths Tinga behind her back.

I nod again, and this time it has nothing to do with what Malcolm's said, but more to do with the implications of what he's said. I mean, if he doesn't really like Tinga, then … No. I don't want to think about it. I'm sure Dad wouldn't hesitate to steal someone else's girlfriend. Which means I can never do such a thing.

But if he's going to dump her, then that's a whole different story. Or at least I think it is.

"Let's take a shower." Malcolm points to a little gazebo-shaped hut off to one side of the pool.

"In there?" I say.

"Yes." He shrugs. "It's the pool house. It's what it's there for."

I don't feel capable of anything. "I might just dry off and get dressed."

"No. You have to get the chlorine out of your hair, otherwise it turns green and falls out."

I can't really argue with this, and I comfort myself with the knowledge that the more time I spend showering, the less time I'll have to spend with Flossie.

I let Malcolm lead me in. He follows, then closes and latches the door behind us.

He rattles the door to make sure it's locked, which seems a little odd. Sure, Tinga and Siggur are around somewhere, but it seems unlikely that either of them would barge straight into a changing room.

On the other hand, if Flossie's on the prowl …

There are nets, brooms, and various floats. Everything smells of hot plastic and chlorine. A narrow shower stall with a fish-patterned curtain is recessed into a corner.

"I'll go first," I say. I rub my belly to try and get rid of an empty feeling.

I step in, pull down my trunks, and twiddle the shower control until a stream of water dribbles out, icy enough to make my teeth hurt.

The water is just turning warm when I hear the curtain pull back and Malcolm steps in behind me. Silly me. I'd assumed that when he'd said, "Let's take a shower," he'd meant that we'd take our showers one after the other.

I expect him to say something about saving hot water, but he doesn't.

I rinse the soap off and move to one side to let him stand under the stream of water. As he brushes past me, I have to confess that even though I don't want to, I can't help looking down. I look up again quickly. Straight into Malcolm's eyes.

"It's okay. You're allowed to look."

I don't really know what to say to this, so I just laugh and say, "Thanks. I don't know if I really need to." There aren't many places I can look in a two-foot-wide shower stall with another male next to me. I take an intense interest in the pattern the hot water makes as it sprays out of the shower head.

"You can even feel it if you like."

Okay, so Malcolm thinks I'm queer too, and he's taunting me.

"Go on. Have a feel," Malcolm says into my ear. "You know you want to."

Now I'm angry. I glare at him.

I'm about to yell *I'm not queer. Let me get out!* But Malcolm's expression disarms me. He has the same toothy grin he had when he first met me at the front door.

Malcolm is queer. He thinks I am and he wants me to touch him.

Invisible hands pull my insides apart. I think I can count the different emotions swirling around inside me.

I want to shove him out of the way and go get dressed.

I want to apologize for not being interested in his penis, and politely ask him to let me out.

I even feel as though perhaps, out of good manners, I should do what he asks.

I should do what he wants because I'm actually kind of curious.

But the feeling that rises to the surface is this: Dad detests homos. In fact, most martial arts people do for some reason. If I'm really cool about Malcolm being gay, then will that make up for the way I've lied and connived my way through the last twenty-four hours? Will it stop me feeling like the son of a storm trooper? A chip off the old block?

"Malcolm." I look him in the face. "I'm sorry. I like you, and respect you, and respect you're a homo, but I'm afraid that I like girls."

Now he looks sarcastic.

"What are you talking about?"

"I'm happy for you to be gay, but I'm afraid I'm not."

"I am not gay!" He pushes me back against the plastic wall of the shower stall, turns off the tap, and tears back the curtain. "You're the one who's been staring at my dick all afternoon."

"That's total rubbish!" My wet feet splatter out onto the wooden floor. "You've been shoving it in my face all afternoon." I grab my towel and wrap it around my waist. "Okay. I got it wrong. You're not gay, but you like showing off."

The doors to the gazebo rattle.

"Malcolm!" shouts Siggur. "Flossie Dog! She needs to walk right now!"

And not a moment too soon.

SIX

When I get home, Hugh's Kawasaki's in the garage but mum's car isn't. I lean the bike against the workbench, shut the garage door, and make my way around the front of the house.

Shrill yells and popping explosions drift out from the open living room window, which means that either Hugh is watching *Doctor Who* or we've been invaded by heavily armed pixies. I peer in through the window. Hugh is stretched out on the living room floor with his back propped up against the sofa. He doesn't see me as he folds an entire half a sandwich into his mouth in one go, then reaches down to the floor for a glass of milk without taking his eyes off the telly. At nearly six foot tall, and with black hair and eyes the color of the Mediterranean in a travel brochure, he'd be a handsome bastard if he had any table manners.

I let myself in through the front door and then poke my head into the living room.

"Humans are inferior. We will destroy them," squawks a dalek on the TV.

"You want a cup of tea?" I don't often ask Hugh for help, but I suppose a little buttering up won't go amiss.

I've seldom seen Hugh move so fast. "A cup of tea?" He does a decent karate sit-up, which means that he pulls his knees into his chest, leans forward, and he's on his feet in a second. I don't know whether to be shocked or impressed. I'm so confused I just stand there in the doorway holding onto the frame. It seems like an overreaction to the offer of tea, and I have just enough time to wonder if he's joined some cult that forbids mention of tea before he's crossed the room and grabbed my forearm.

"I'll tell you what I want." He twists my arm behind my back and then grabs my other wrist. "I want to know where my magazine is." Realization slaps me around the face as he lifts my feet right off the ground and propels me into the living room.

Girls on Parade! Oh, crap.

First Line of Defense: Denial. "I don't know what you're talking about." With my hands out of action, I twist my hips and throw a back kick at the top of Hugh's leg, or at least I try. Somehow his leg isn't where I expect it to be. Why do I always shut my eyes when Hugh attacks me?

"Exterminate," continues the dalek as I notice the sofa rushing up to meet me. "Destroy all humans."

"Have you been going through my things?"

My face is pushed into a flowery cushion, and something hard, painful, and very reminiscent of a knee is planted between my shoulder blades.

Second Line of Defense: Protest. "Let me go!"

"I want to know where my magazine is first."

Third Line of Defense: Bargain. "I won't tell you unless you let me go first."

Hugh presses harder and it begins to hurt.

"I can't breathe."

"What a shame," says Hugh. "Not being able to breathe is something of a drawback these days." He presses his knee even harder into my back.

I really can't breathe, but in trying to reduce the pressure of his knee in my back, I find a small gap between the cushion and something that feels—and in fact tastes—a lot like a TV remote. "I really can't breathe," I mumble. "I'll suffocate and then you'll never find the magazine, plus *Mother!* will be furious." Which is probably a lot of words for someone who's using his last breath, but then it is in the heat of the moment.

"Oh dear." Hugh twists my arms farther. "A small price to pay."

I go limp and take tiny sips of air in through my nose, in the hope that it looks like I've stopped breathing and passed out.

"Jay." Hugh pulls my arms back. "Stop pissing around." Then he makes his first blunder. He relaxes his grip.

I jerk my arms out of his fingers and flip onto my back.

I'm just about to say, "Nah. Fooled you!" when my left heel swings up and makes contact with Hugh. Right in the bollocks.

Hugh makes a sound a little like a cow that hasn't been milked for a couple of days, then he leaps into the air, stumbles back against the wall, and sinks down to the carpet.

"Sorry. *Sorry!*" I shout. Not so much because I'm filled with regret for setting back his reproductive plans, but more because I'm afraid of his counter-attack, and I want him to be fully aware that I only kicked him in the nuts by accident.

"Bloody hell, Jason. That was uncalled for."

Hugh never calls me by my full name unless he's really angry with me, or I've hurt his feelings. On this occasion I think I might have done both.

"Well, what do you expect? You were going to kill me."

"You went through my things."

"You were going to kill me over a magazine."

"Jay." Hugh screws up his face like he has a bad headache. "It's not just the magazine." He waves his hand as if he's swatting an invisible fly. "Oh, never mind."

"I was going to buy you another copy. You'd have a new one." I maneuver myself so I'm sitting up on the sofa, and I rotate my shoulders which are now sore. "You'd be better off. I was going to do you a favor." I stop. At this point even I don't believe what I'm saying.

Hugh rolls onto his knees then sits back on his heels. "Have you started training again?"

"No. Don't be daft."

"Really. Because when you punch you punch like Granny Smallfield"—Hugh slides a hand down the front of his jeans—

"but that back kick you just did is almost dangerous." He pulls his hand out, sniffs his fingers, then puts it back. "That wasn't one bit brotherly."

"Brotherly!"

A loud bang comes from the TV as a dalek's head explodes. There's a cut to the Doctor saying, "Well, I think that worked quite splendidly."

"I came to you for advice, and you tried to murder me. Is that brotherly?"

"Let me get this straight. You actually want *me* to apologize?" Hugh leans back against the wall and pulls his knees into his chest. "You invade my privacy. You steal—"

"Borrow."

"Oh, forget I said anything. What did you want my advice on? Gary Palma will sell you another *Girls on Parade*."

"I know that. I think every fourteen-year-old in Port Agnes-on-Sea knows that."

"You have to pay for advice. Amuse me," says Hugh. "Tell me what happened to the *Girls on Parade*."

I sketch out the main points. "I tore it—by accident— so I threw it away, then went to buy you another one. I got all the way to Palma's but then I just forgot to actually buy the magazine."

"I don't really understand." Hugh squints through one eye as if he's aiming a rifle at me. "How could you go for a three-mile bike ride and forget what you went for in the first place?"

I blow out a long ragged breath. Maybe I should just tell him everything. "I met a girl at Palma's. She invited me to her blue-belt test in three weeks, and she expects me to spar, and I haven't trained for over two years. I'm going to get my arse presented to me on a silver platter."

Hugh nods slowly. "You know, boys—or young men—in your situation often like to ask a girl for her phone number."

"Look. I don't want advice on what I didn't do. I want advice on what I should do now."

Hugh shrugs.

It's now or never. "You're a black belt." Oh, man. Do I sound whiny sometimes! "You can train me one-on-one. You can get me in shape in three weeks."

Now Hugh shakes his head. "There are black belts and there are black belts. There are the ones who can kill you with a well-aimed blow from a hard-bristle toothbrush, and there are the ones who get their belts for showing up to class on time. I'm one of the latter sorts."

Now I'm on my feet. "But you could still train me. You have the skills, and you know what I need to know." I swing my arms back, then shoot them forward and step into a fighting stance. "*Kee-yah!*"

"Jay, I think it's time you got down off your high horse, and just went and asked the one person you should ask to help you with this."

"Are you out of your mind?" Dad would be the very last person I would ask for help with anything. He doesn't even know how to be a dad!

"Listen to yourself. I didn't even mention a name and you know who I mean." Hugh pulls himself to his feet, dusts off his jeans, then retrieves his glass of milk from the table and drains it. "I know what you think of him." He points the glass at me. "Just stop and hear me out for a moment. You're persecuting that man for no good reason. You have this lopsided view of our family history. I don't think that things happened quite the way you think they did."

"So how?"

"Just trust me. I think that sometimes these things happen for a reason, and maybe this is the time for you to bury the hatchet with Dad."

"I don't know if I can do it."

"Jay. It's a means to an end. Train with him. Get this girl, and then go back to hating him if you want."

"You don't care if I get a girlfriend or not. I don't suppose there's anything in it for you."

"Are you pulling my leg? Of course I want you to have a girlfriend. If you had a girlfriend, you'd be less likely to go through my magazine collection." Hugh crashes down onto the sofa. "Look. Jay, there is one thing to think about. I'm not any kind of expert in these things, but this girl *merely* invited you to her blue-belt test. She didn't ask about your availability for marriage. If you're really feeling strongly about Dad, and karate, and storm troopers, why not just forget the whole thing?"

I sit down at the opposite end of the sofa and stare at my knees.

"I like her. She's really nice." An image of a smiling Tinga floats into my head. "She has teeth."

"Teeth?"

"And everything else as well."

"Jay. I have no doubt that you're head over heels for her, but how do you know she likes you?" The end credits roll for *Doctor Who*. "I mean, it seems to me that if she really likes you, she might want to see you again before three weeks are up." Hugh digs around between the cushions, pulls out the remote, and mutes the TV.

"I know it doesn't make sense, but you'd have to be there to know."

"But, Jay." Hugh throws the remote on the coffee table, then wipes his hand. I must have dribbled on it. The back snaps off the remote and the batteries roll onto the carpet. "All joking aside, she didn't give you her phone number or anything?"

"I think her parents are kind of weird and don't like her having a boyfriend. She didn't give me a number because she doesn't want me calling."

Hugh gets down on his hands and knees to look for the batteries. "But you like her and you would see her tomorrow if you could, wouldn't you?"

"I could go and see her any day I wanted."

"Let me get this straight. You can see her any time you want and you're going to leave it for three weeks?"

"Well. No. She told me she walks her dog at four o'clock every day in the park, but she didn't invite me to walk the dog with her."

"Jay." Hugh stands up, this time placing the remote back on the coffee table. "She probably told you where she walks the dog because she wants you to go there and meet her. Did she tell you the name of the park?"

"Wish Park."

Hugh flops back onto the couch and pulls a sour face. "That's a long way. Shame it's not closer, but I suppose you can't have everything."

"And she told me twice."

"She told you twice? Jay! How dense can you get? If she told you twice then she really wants you to go."

"Well, how am I supposed to know that?"

"Is she pretty?"

"Yes."

"Does she have nice tits?" Hugh makes a gesture so vile I won't even describe it.

"Hugh! Is that all you think about?"

"Is there something else I ought to think about?" Hugh folds his arms into his armpits. "But does she? It's important."

"I don't know."

"But she was right in front of you."

"I didn't look."

"Wait a minute. There was a pair of breasts right in front of you and you didn't look at them?"

"I didn't think about it," I say. "I was looking at her face. I was even at a swimming pool with her and I didn't look."

Hugh sits sideways and gives me a searching look. "You're not one of those *homosexuals*, are you?" He says the word *homosexuals* in a silly upper-class accent.

I can do no more than roll my eyes. I really can't.

"In that case, Jay, it's obvious that you are fatally besotted with this girl. Sell all your possessions. Give up going to school if you have to. Go and see Dad and ask him to train you every night one-on-one. Go to Wish Park at four o'clock, because you will know no peace until this girl is yours."

SEVEN

So here I am again, staring at my storm-trooper dad from my shadowy archway on the opposite side of Trafalgar Street.

About a dozen blokes and two girls stand in ranks and bow to my dad inside the dojo.

"*Hooss!*" The shout reverberates across to me. The class is over. A few moments later the students pour out of the door. Mostly silent, they head in different directions. Each has a different style of jacket and backpack, but all have identical baggy white trousers that will indicate to anyone watching that they have come from a karate class and should not be trifled with.

I count to sixty after the last one leaves. I cross the street, pass the storm trooper, and let myself into the now-empty studio. I kick off my shoes and chuck them next to a pair of walking boots. Then I bow and bellow "*Hooss!*" as loud as I can.

The office door opens almost immediately, and for the first time in over two years, I'm face-to-face with him. He's big, but somehow not as big as he was. He's also thinner, and his hair looks blacker than I remember.

I expect him to make some smart-arse remark like *Look what the cat dragged in,* but he doesn't say anything. He just looks surprised and sad. Sad enough to cry, and that makes the tears prick behind my eyes.

"Jason," he says. He crosses the dojo in a couple of strides, lifts my feet off the floor, and clasps me into his chest. His stubbly cheek scratches the top of my head, and I smell coffee and some kind of aftershave.

As far as I can remember, he's never hugged me before. He's not the huggy type. It occurs to me that I should make a point of seeing him regularly from now on, just to discourage him from ever hugging me again.

"Are you hungry?" He plants me back onto the floor. "There's a new Indian place just opened in Cromwell Road and I hear it's very good."

"Um…" Even though I hate everything he stands for, and I have no respect for him, he looks so delighted that I almost can't bear to turn down his offer. But I have to. I'm not here to eat. I'm here to train. A tiny trickle of fear crawls up my back, and for the first time I realize that I hadn't even considered the possibility that he might just say *No.*

I blurt it out before I can think too much. "I want to start training again."

"Fantastic." He doesn't miss a beat. It's as if this was the very thing he was expecting me to ask, and his grin is wider if anything. He steps towards me. *Please, no more hugs*. But he just grips my shoulders. The sharp knuckles rise up from the back of his hands like a row of pyramids. "You know I was just thinking about you this afternoon."

Now he looks all weepy again.

Please don't go all sentimental and American on me!

He shakes his head. "I can't begin to tell you how happy this makes me." He is going to go all American. He probably gets it from all the Yanks he hangs around with on film sets.

"I had such great hopes for you," he says. "I was totally gutted when you stopped training."

"Good, because I was totally *gutted* when you left home." Wait a minute. Did I just say that? I brace myself for a slap at the very least. I have another squint at his big knuckles, but he leaves his hand on my shoulder. He gives me the same look he once gave me the time we were sparring and I hit him with my first really hard back kick. Only on this occasion he doesn't laugh it off, he just folds his lips over his teeth.

"I'm sorry," he says. "I made a bit of a mess of things. I wish there was something I could do to make it up to you."

I'm getting in the mood for answering him. I want to tell him that what's done is done, and you can't put the genie back in the bottle, but I bite my lip. Instead I tell him, "There is something."

"Fire away. Tell me."

"I want you to train me one-on-one. I want to start right now. I want to be fighting fit in twenty days."

He gives me the exact same aiming-the-rifle look that

Hugh gave me earlier, and I can take a fair guess at what's scrolling through his head. Reasons why he can't do it one-on-one and that I'll have to join a class; reasons why he can't do it now; reasons why it's impossible for me to be ready to fight in such a short time. I'm so certain he's going to give me a list of excuses that I almost jump when he says, "Alright." He nods a couple of times, then turns from side to side as if he's looking for something. "Just put your jacket with your shoes for now."

I throw it in the corner with my shoes.

He takes a step back, bends forward from the waist, and shouts, "*Hooss!*"

"*Hooss!*" I reply. I bow and place my feet shoulder-width apart. I clench my fists in front of my groin and it all floods back. The kicks, the punches, the katas, and best of all, the sparring. If I half-close my eyes I can turn the dojo into our back garden. My hair prickles. How could I have stopped doing this?

Dad shoves something at me. A cord with two gray handles. Right. A jump rope. I'd forgotten the warming-up part.

"Let's just start with three minutes this evening."

I take hold of the handles, swing the rope back over my head, and let it rest against my calves. "Ready."

I rise up on the balls of my feet and take a deep breath. "Jump!"

Straight away he turns his back on me and retreats into his office.

I swing the rope. On the first couple of turns the rope hits my shins; then I go for three or four turns before it stings my toes. "Ouch!"

Then I get going. The rope whines as it cuts through the air making a sphere around me, but my guts slop as I jump. Twenty. Thirty. My chest tightens and my forearms scream. It's a weighted rope. For the love of God, couldn't he have given me a light one for my first session in two years?

I keep going. The room swims. I can't breathe. Can a fourteen-year-old have a heart attack? I don't want to stop, but on one turn my feet land back on the ground, and it's as if someone's put Super Glue on the mat. There is no way I can lift my feet again. I lean forward and rest my hands on my knees.

He's right in front of me. He must have been listening from the office for this very moment, but I have to give him his due. There's no smug grin on his face. He has what is about as close to no expression as a person can get. "Two and a half minutes," he says.

"Thank goodness for that. Only half a minute left."

"No," he says. "You've done thirty seconds. You have two and a half minutes remaining. Jump!"

Somehow I get through the next two and a half minutes one or two jumps at a time. Next I do three push-ups, five accordion sit-ups, and about ten really lame jumping jacks. Then I do it all over again, only worse.

When I get down on my hands and knees to pick up the jump rope for the third time, he says, "I think that's enough warm-up for tonight. Hang up the rope and come back."

I limp over to the wall and hook the rope up with the others.

"How do you feel?"

"Fantastic," I blurt out between long gasps for air.

I stagger back to my spot in front of him.

"When was the last time you trained?"

"Two years. Almost to the day."

"No dizziness? Chest pain?"

I shake my head.

"Oh, to be fourteen again," he says. He spreads his feet out. "Let's do a little light stretching. Mirror me."

I step my right foot out so it's opposite his left foot. I bend my leg and twist towards the mirrored right wall.

"Don't force it," he says. "Count to ten."

"One … two … three …"

"Counting to ten?" He twists to face me. "Have you forgotten?"

And I haven't. It's all stored away somewhere. *"Ichi … ni … san … shi … go … roku … shichi … hachi …"*

"Very good," he says. "If you can remember that, then there's a good chance you remember quite a lot of the other stuff as well."

Very good? A tingle runs across my shoulders and up my neck. I know my face is bright red.

How long has it been since anyone has told me I'm good at anything?

We do some more leg stretches, followed by some toe touching and arm stretches, all in silence except for my counting in Japanese. As I'm stretching, the tingle in my neck begins to spread across my back and down my arms. At first I think the tingle has something to do with the stretching. Then it dawns on me that for the last twenty-four hours—

since I met Tinga—everything I've done, I've done with the feeling that it's all a lost cause anyway.

But now, even in just the last few minutes, I've started to have this suspicion. The suspicion is not so much that it's all going to work. I don't think I would go that far. The suspicion is more that there's no longer any reason that it couldn't work.

I'm training and, as Dad pointed out, if I can still count in Japanese then I can probably remember a lot of the moves.

Malcolm doesn't want to go out with Tinga anymore, and Tinga likes me.

I can go and see her at the park. Somehow I will get there.

The whole scheme really isn't impossible.

"Okay." Dad drops a black tote bag at my feet. "Let's move on." He must have got it out of the office while I was lost in thought. He squats down and pulls red-colored gloves, shin guards, and head gear out of the bag. "Let's see what you really remember."

"We're going to spar?"

Dad smirks at me. I know he's thinking about a sarcy comeback. Obviously we're going to spar. He didn't drag all this gear out just to play dress up. I don't know why I said anything. Then his face softens.

"We don't have to if you don't think you're ready."

Of course I'm not ready. I feel empty, and my heart is pounding again, but I don't say anything. I sit on the floor, pull out a shin guard, and fasten it onto my leg. I hope that is a good enough answer, because I don't think I can say anything right now.

"Good man."

The tingle again.

He slides head gear onto my head and fastens the strap under my chin. "Too tight?" he says.

I fasten the other shin guard, then rock the head gear up and down.

Dad grabs my arms one at a time and slides gloves onto my hands.

He puts the tote over by the wall. I no longer feel like me. I bounce a couple of times on my toes, and shake out my shoulders. I'm not Jay any more. I'm a warrior. I turn my head to look at myself in the mirror and immediately wish I hadn't.

I'm still me. I'm just Jay in a bunch of toy armor. I don't look like a ninja warrior. I just look like a kid who's put on someone else's sparring gear for a laugh. But that's not the worst of it. The armor reminds me of something, but I can't quite put my finger on it.

"Let's go," says Dad. He of course is just in his *gi*. No armor.

As a high-ranking black belt, he would not even consider that I could hurt him, or that he would hurt me. I swing my arms back, then forward into my stance. "*Kee-yah!*"

I crouch as low as I can, then circle Dad. I try to focus my gaze on his eyes, but he stares me out in a second and I look at his chest. I want him to start. I want him to throw a punch or a kick. Something I can react to. It's like opening a conversation with someone who doesn't want to talk. He just circles the dojo opposite me.

Are two minutes going to run out without any punches or kicks?

I aim a side kick at his mid-section, but he catches my foot, swings it off to the side, then slaps the back of my head gear with a *pop*.

Now I'm puffing. My breathing is loud in the head gear. One lame kick and I'm done. I swing a roundhouse at his chin, but he leans back, my foot swings past his face, and I spin into a back kick. My foot goes way off to the side. He steps in and slaps the back of my head gear, in exactly the same spot.

If I can't hit him, I might as well try something wild. I bounce twice on my toes, then twist into a jump-back kick. My foot flies out and hits something solid. As I land, Dad takes a step back out of reach. He pulls up his pants and tightens his belt.

I got him. I really *got* him. A millisecond later he slides in. There's a huge fist, and a flash of pain right in the center of my forehead.

He grabs my shoulders. "Are you alright?"

Kee-yah! I crouch back into my stance.

"Jay!" He clasps his hands over my fists, and pushes them down. "You are a ninja, but that's enough for the first session."

I slump onto the floor as if I've been standing for hours, and unfasten all the gear. Dad packs it away.

He asks me about going to the Indian place again, but

I turn him down. It really is enough for the first session. It's enough for my first training session, and it's also enough for my first meeting with Dad. I put on my jacket and shoes. I stop in the doorway, shout "*Hooss,*" and bow.

"Jay," he says. He steps out of the door with me and stands on the pavement in his bare feet. "Have a hot bath when you get back. You haven't trained for two years, so you're going to be really stiff tomorrow, but a hot bath will help."

"Can I come back at the same time tomorrow?" I say.

"No." He turns and steps back into the doorway. "I know you're in a hurry to get in shape, but you have to rest after your first day. If you don't rest, you'll overdo it and get some kind of injury that could stop you training for months."

"Okay." I know I can't argue with him, and I know he's probably right. "Saturday then."

"Fantastic," he says. He steps all the way in, closes the door, and waves at me through the glass.

Just that gesture stirs something in me. I can't figure out what it is exactly. It's like déjà vu. Like the way he's waving is something he did when I was a kid—obviously, I'm still a kid now—and I was too young to remember him doing it, but the wave is kind of in there somewhere. Like the Japanese counting. Just for a moment I feel like we've switched places. I'm in the dojo looking out at me, and I get a glimpse of what he's lost, and how he feels about it. I just stand there and look in at him, lift my hand, and wave back.

I shake my head to get rid of the thoughts, then turn

and set off for home. The cold night air and walking bring me back to the here and now, and the feeling that I can read Dad's mind is replaced by the feeling of his big knuckle, which I can still feel in the middle of my forehead.

EIGHT

By the time I get home, I'm too tired to take a bath. I barely have enough energy to pull my clothes off and climb into bed. I lie there and think about my big scheme. There are so many things that could go wrong, but it could really work. I start thinking about how I could get the bus to Wish Park tomorrow, and I actually get on the bus, but there's a problem right away. The bus driver is Tinga's dad. Don't ask me how I know this fact, but I do. Not only is he Tinga's dad, but he knows who I am and why I'm taking the bus. Instead of driving to Wish Park, like he's supposed to, he drives down the Clifton Docks and onto a ferry bound for Belgium.

Next thing I know, the sun is streaming through the curtains. I don't think I've moved all night because when I try to shift my leg, a dull ache runs right up to my armpit. I wince for a second, then stop because it hurts my forehead. Somehow I manage to ease myself off the bed and into the bathroom. Is it possible that nobody bothered to wake me up for fifty years? I check the mirror, but I'm still fourteen. I'm going to have to restyle my hair to hide the red, knuckle-shaped dot in the middle of my forehead, otherwise it looks like I've joined some Eastern religion.

I walk down the hill to get the bus. Even though I'm the fourteen-year-old me, I can't walk any faster than a sixty-four-year-old with my rigid legs. Before I'm halfway to the bus stop, I know I'm not going to make it in time. I hear a buzz of bearings and a bike zips past. I don't need another hint. I retrace my steps, haul my bike out from behind *Mother!*'s car, raise the saddle, and give it its second airing in two years.

Now that I'm not banging my knees on the handle-bars, riding is actually easier than walking for some reason. I have to admit that the saddle isn't as comfortable as it could be, but you can't have everything. In fact, riding helps me loosen up a bit, so by the time I get to school I can actually walk okay.

While I'm riding, I figure out that I can ride to Wish Park as well. Not only will it be much quicker, but biking has another big advantage over the bus, which is that I can stop worrying that my dream about Tinga's dad was some kind of premonition. It would just be too weird. If I'm going to have a prophetic dream, I hope it's going to reveal something more earth-shattering than the fact that my possible future girlfriend's dad is a bus driver.

I can't really stay focused for more than three seconds at a time at school, but as soon as we're let out, I freewheel the bike out to Westbourne Street. It's like the bike has a mind of its own. The front wheel turns right instead of left. West instead of east. To Wish Park instead of home. I stand up on the pedals and pump my legs. As I ride, I convince myself that it was fate that made me take the bike this morning. I mean, it has to be a gamble. Hugh might be right. Tinga might be there at the park at four, and she might be happy to see me. He might also be wrong. Tinga might be there, but she might not be happy to see me. Or I might have picked a day when Malcolm turns up to see her, which would be weird.

Wish Park is about three miles along the seafront from the school, in the opposite direction from home. Two hours to walk both ways, probably two hours on the bus, but only half an hour extra by bike. I don't know if it's worth the gamble, but it is exercise, and if Dad's right, then the exercise won't do me any harm.

I get to the park early. I make a leisurely lap of the park to see if I can spot her, but it doesn't offer much. I ride past a football game. Twenty-two blokes running after a ball. They seem pretty sure of what they're doing. Most of the spectators on the touch-line are women—wives and girl-friends—but some of them are probably my age.

I cruise past the playground. Mums and little kids are all crammed on one end by the swings. There are two girls sitting on the roundabout in dark red Cardinal Newman uniforms. I know neither of them is Tinga, but I can't resist looking.

I let the bike freewheel and crane my neck backwards.

"Hoy!"

I swing around to the front just in time to see three figures a couple of feet in front of me. I slam on the anchors, the back tire slides, and I miss them by inches, noting as I pass that they are three skinheads. They all have their bovver boots—tall army boots with white laces. They have tight bleach-spattered jeans held up with red braces, and check shirts with the sleeves rolled up over their biceps.

Something tells me not to stop, but I let the bike roll forward, then pull up a few yards ahead of them.

"Sorry about that." I touch my foot to the ground.

"You missed me by that much." The biggest one, who has a narrow face, holds his thumb and forefinger an inch apart. "Wanker!"

"Stupid arsehole," says one of the shorter ones.

The three of them stand in line, then walk towards me.

That's it.

Adrenaline shoots down my arms and legs. I stand up on the pedals and start to pump as hard as I can. I don't even pause to change up. The bike pulses forward and the tires swish on the tarmac. I want to put as much park between them and me as I can.

Running feet clatter behind me. Boots with metal toes. A hand grabs my shoulder, pulling me off to the side. Without thinking, I windmill my arm and it breaks the grip. Like counting in Japanese. Something else I didn't know I remembered. I pump the pedals again.

"Queer!" The clattering boots slow to a walking pace behind me, but I don't slow down until I'm at Marine Parade.

My heart is pounding a thousand beats a minute.

When I look around, I half expect to see Narrow-face sprinting towards me, but there's only a couple of old biddies with a Pekingese, and I think even I could deal with them if they decide to attack.

My shirt is soaked with sweat under my backpack. I freewheel to the curb, prop the bike up with my foot, and stick my nose close to my armpit. *Fantastic.* I'll just have to make sure I stay downwind of Tinga. That is, if I see her.

Next to the park, just across the street, is a café. What attracts my attention is an afghan hound tied up outside. One afghan hound looks much like another, but I would guess that this one is Flossie, which means that Malcolm is inside and I really did pick the wrong day.

Maybe I should just turn around and go home.

On the other hand, I've come all this way to see Tinga. I want to see her even if I do have to share her with Malcolm.

I lock my bike to the opposite railing to Flossie. I don't want Flossie to slobber on my bike.

Malcolm's not in the café. For half a second I think he might be in the toilet or something. Then I see a girl sitting in the booth by the window, but facing inward so she doesn't see me. She digs around in her handbag, pulls out a long white cigarette, pops it into her mouth, and then pulls out a disposable lighter.

"Hi, Siggur," I say.

She tears the unlit cigarette out of her mouth and throws it back into the bag.

She presents me with her finest scowl.

"It's okay. I don't care if you smoke, and I won't tell

anyone." She looks sad rather than angry, and I can't stop myself from grinning as if I'm the older of the two of us.

She takes in a little breath as if she's inhaling an invisible cigarette. She doesn't say anything, but her scowl softens to a neutral look. Maybe I could do a trade with her. She probably needs English conversation. I need practice talking to girls. She has to be at least sixteen or seventeen. I'm way too young for her, so she's safe. She's not potential-girlfriend material.

"I was going to get tea," I say, separating each word. I point to the seat opposite her. "Could I sit with you?"

"Of course, but I'm expecting a friend."

This is about ten degrees warmer than the scowl.

She walks her hand over to her bag and pulls out the cigarette again. It's bent. She holds it up between us like an exhibit. She squints through one eye and straightens it.

I buy my tea and slide into the corner of the booth opposite from her. I crumple myself low down into the seat as if I'm still hiding from the skinheads. I'm not sure she's really into the idea of sharing a table with me, but when she exhales her smoke she seems to be careful to blow it away from me.

My knee bounces up and down so I put my hand on it. I have no idea what to talk to girls about, but I know what to talk to foreigners about.

"Where are you from?"

"Our house in Denmark." It's the first time I've seen her smile.

That's sweet. I like her English-isms. She flicks her ash into the saucer of her empty coffee cup.

"Are you from Copenhagen?"

Her smile gets big enough that I actually see a flash of her teeth.

She draws an imaginary map on the table. "No, silly boy. I'm from the city of Aarhus." She stabs her finger next to her cup. "It's about fifty kilometers from Kovenhaagn." She slides her finger over to my cup. "I live there with my mother and older brother."

"Oh, that's funny. I live with my mother and older brother, too."

This statement kills the conversation for a minute. We're going to have to move beyond the bounds of small talk if we're going to discuss why neither of us have dads who live at home.

She smokes while I drink my tea. I try to think of how to phrase the next question without seeming to pry. It's Siggur who breaks the silence. "I don't want to be nosey, but why no dad?" She stubs her cigarette, but continues to inhale as if she's smoking.

Must be a Danish thing.

"My parents separated a couple years ago; now my father lives with his mother." This is true, and it's the reason I can no longer visit Granny Smallfield.

"Oh, that's pathetic." She covers her mouth. "I'm sorry. I didn't mean to insult your dad, but it's like he's still a boy and can't make a go of things by himself."

"My gran's pretty old." I take a sip of tea. "She's almost eighty—and she was ill at the time."

"Oh. I see." Siggur reddens.

I wish I hadn't told her that. The last thing I want to do is make her feel bad.

The second to last thing I want to do is to defend Dad, and I'm almost making him out to be some kind of saint for leaving home to nurse his little white-haired mother.

"No." I turn the cup around in its saucer. "Actually, I don't know how ill she really was, and anyway she's okay now."

"But still." Siggur takes another cigarette-less inhale. "At that age she probably needs help."

I shake my head. "You know how people tell you stuff, and you just accept it as the truth, then you repeat it without thinking?"

"Yes." Siggur actually laughs, and I get the same kind of tingle in my shoulders I got last night at the dojo. "I know that feeling perfectly well," she says. She points her finger at me. "You think you're telling the truth, but you're not. Sort of a second-hand lie."

"Right." I drain my tea down to the sugary gloop at the bottom of the cup. "That's exactly what it is." I sit up straight. "So the long and short of it is that I don't know if he really does live there."

"We were going to have a nice English tea-time chat, and we're talking of such important things."

Now it's my turn to laugh.

"I don't know. It's still sad." Siggur sits back in her seat and puts her hands in her lap. "How old are you? Thirteen? Fourteen? Your parents should tell you the truth about this type of thing."

"*Thirteen!* Thanks a bunch. I'm fourteen." I look down into my teacup as if I can read my fortune, but it's tea-bag tea. No leaves. Nothing to read my fortune by. "To be honest, it's probably up to me to find out more about my dad, but I don't really like talking about him." There are no leaves in the cup, but there is melted sugar. "By the way, I'll be fifteen next March."

"My birthday is March, too. Which day?"

"The eighteenth." I dip my finger into my cup to scoop out the sugar, like I always do. Then I stop. This is not the time.

"That's okay," she says. "If you don't tell about my smoking, I won't tell about you putting your dirty finger in your teacup."

"Deal." I wipe my sugary finger on my jacket and put out my hand to shake hers.

She makes a disgusted face, but it's a joke. She smiles again, clasps my hand, and squeezes it for a moment. Her hand is warm and she has a tiny thumbnail.

"I'm the third of March. We're both Pisces." She scrunches out her cigarette. "You must be an artist. Pisces are always artists."

"No. Not really." I want to ask her how old she is. I want to tell her I don't believe in horoscopes, but Flossie howls from outside.

Siggur looks up and says something like, "*Hey Any-edah!*"

I twist around just in time to see a woman in her twenties closing the door behind her.

Siggur stands up and the two of them hug and kiss, then they pull back and gabble in what I presume must be Danish, then they hug each other again. I wonder what it must be like for two girls to hug when they both have boobs.

Does it feel like anything?

I realize I've forgotten all about Tinga. I should go back to the park. I might have missed her while I've been sitting here.

"Bye, Siggur," I say.

Siggur breaks away for a moment. "Bye-bye, Jay." She actually gives me a big smile. "It was nice speaking with you."

Then she spreads her arms out towards me.

My heart pounds. For one moment I actually think she's going to give me a hug.

I am actually going to feel a pair of female breasts pressed against me.

"It was nice speaking to you, too." I cough and clear my throat, then put my hands out to Siggur. She does this thing where she leans her shoulders forward and arches her middle back, because she crushes me into her neck, but our chests don't make contact.

Mind you, her neck is nice. Her shoulders are round and soft, and her hair is every bit as smooth and silky as they tell you it's going to be on the commercials.

NINE

I can't have been in the café for more than fifteen minutes. Tinga could still be around, so I might as well do another lap of the park and see if I can spot her.

Bugger and blast! The tea gave me a burst of energy, but the down side is that I've got to take a leak. There's plenty of clumps of shrubs and bushes, but with my luck I'd be exposed and in midstream when Rosko came sniffing around. Either that or I'd choose the clump the skinheads are lurking in, because they don't seem to be anywhere else.

Only one thing for it. There's a low brick pavilion on the slope behind the playground. The middle part of the building is a shelter, but it has a door on either end that look like toilets. I stand on the pedals for a high viewpoint, then inch forward. No skinheads. When I reach the playground, I put on some speed to get up the slope. A movement from inside the shelter catches my eye.

Three people fighting. No. Not fighting. Maybe playing at fighting, and I recognize one of them.

I slam on the brakes, but they give a yelp like a dog that's had its tail trodden on. Three heads swivel in my direction. *Bugger and blast.* They've seen me. Too late to just pass them by.

They're no skinheads, but maybe this is worse.

Malcolm and two girls are sort of huddled on the long bench that runs around the inside of the shelter. I can't stop staring at the girls. Surely if Malcolm's with them, then one of them must be Tinga, but neither of them looks much like her. Maybe she's done something to her hair and she looks different. I know girls can sometimes do that. I look from one to the other, but neither of them is her.

Right now they're just sitting there staring at me, but what were they doing just before they saw me? Were the girls tickling him?

Since our shower, I've been laboring under the impression that Malcolm's gay. Would someone who was gay play around with girls like that? More to the point, would a bloke with a girlfriend get all touchy-feely with two girls who were not his girlfriend? Now I'm really confused. But now he's seen me and I have to at least say hello. Maybe I'm seeing this all wrong.

"What'cha, Malc," I say between breaths. Pedaling up a steep, grassy slope—especially after you've stopped halfway—is not the easiest thing in the world.

Malcolm jumps up. "Jay!" he says, drawing out the *a.* "What on earth are you doing down here?"

Good question. What am I doing here?

He ambles out of the shelter towards me. He's wearing a black Harrington jacket and his white *gi* trousers. He must be on his way to the dojo. "You should have rung me." He sounds friendly enough, but something about the way he jumped up makes me think he's not overjoyed to see me. "Told me you were coming."

One of the girls appears behind Malcolm. "You got a light, mate?" she says to me. She's one of the Cardinal Newman girls I saw earlier. She has her blond hair cut in one of those styles that's spiky on top and long at the sides.

"No. Sorry. I don't smoke."

The other girl comes up behind her. "You're not much use, are you?"

"No," I say. Just for a moment I wish I did smoke. The second girl is tall with dark brown hair tied back in a ponytail. She's pretty. I'd probably fancy her if I wasn't so obsessed with Tinga. I wish I smoked because I want her to think I'm cool and grown up, and she's looking at me like I'm an annoying kid of about five.

Maybe I should just go and play on the swings.

"What brings you over here?" says Malcolm.

"Are you two mates?" says the tall one. She looks over at Malcolm, then back at me like she's seeing if we look like we could really be friends.

"You going to introduce us or what?" asks the spiky one. Then she looks past me towards the playground. "Hey chief, you got a light?"

I glance over my shoulder. A bloke in a shiny gray suit is headed for the men's toilet. He ignores her.

"This is Jay," says Malcolm. "This is Julie." He points to the spiky one, then puts his hand on the taller one's triceps. "And this is Julia."

"Hi, Julie," I say to the spiky one. Or maybe she's Julia. Why don't I make a better job of listening when people tell me their names. "Hi." I nod to the other one.

"Bit confusing, isn't it," says the taller one. "If it makes it easier you can call me Julia and her Stinky-Winky."

"Or," says the spiky one, "you can call me Julie and her Warty-Webster."

There's a rattling noise behind me. I spin around. The bloke in the business suit is holding up a box of matches.

"Here," he says, and coughs.

"You got some smokes as well?" says the spiky one.

"What?" says the business bloke. "Four cigarettes?"

"No," says the spiky one. "Just for me and her." Then she glances at me. "Unless you smoke, Jay." She says this in a sweet voice, as if she's speaking to a child.

I know I'm going red. "No." I shrug.

The bloke doesn't offer the pack to the girls, but gives them each a cigarette, lights them, then hurries into the toilet as if he's worried he's about to be shaken down for something else.

Malcolm asks the spiky one, "Are you really called Stinky-Winky?"

"Oh yeah," says the tall one, taking a long puff of her

smoke. "There was this bloke doing a washing machine demo down in Churchill Square."

"Oh stop," says the spiky one, but she giggles as if she doesn't really want her friend to stop.

"Anyway, the bloke was saying, *Bring me your dirtiest laundry*, and all these mums were giving him shirts..."

"And bras," says the spiky one.

"And bras," repeats the tall one, "and stuff like that. The bloke dips the clothes into the machine for a few seconds, then pulls them out clean. And he's saying, *Into the wash, out of the wash*. Each time he pulls something out of the machine he puts it under his nose and says, *Under the nose, fresh as a rose*. Then Julie's mum gives him a pair of Julie's panties. He dips them into his machine and he goes, *Into the wash, out of the wash*, then he puts it under his nose and goes, *Into the wash, out of the wash; into the wash, out of the wash; into the wash, out of the wash*."

By this point both girls have collapsed onto the bench in hysterics, but neither of them is sitting next to Malcolm.

I feel rude, but I can't laugh. I've never heard the word *winky* used in that way before. I can't believe the tall one would say such personal things about the spiky one. I can't believe they would say it in front of Malcolm and me. Are they somehow open and relaxed with Malcolm because he's gay, and they feel safe with him?

The spiky one glances at me and whispers something to the tall one.

"Have to go for a short walk," says the tall one.

Both girls stand up and rush past me to the women's toilet.

And it's just me and Malcolm. I prop my bike up, crash out on the bench opposite him, and rub my tingling legs.

"So, Jay," says Malcolm. "What brings you over to these parts?" He steps back into the shelter and flops down on the wooden bench that runs around the inside wall.

"I just fancied a ride," I say. "Where's Tinga?"

"Tinga?" The smile vanishes from his face. "She doesn't usually come over to this end of the park. You can't bring dogs here."

"How do you know Julie and Julia?" I force a big grin as I say this so the question doesn't sound like, *Why aren't you with Tinga?*

He laughs. "They're in my class." He leans forward and puts his elbows on his knees. "Julia—the taller one—she's nice, right?"

"Right."

He glances off to the side and whispers to me, "I quite like her."

I'm about to ask him exactly what he means when a voice behind me says, "So, what school do you go to?" The tall one flops down on the bench between me and Malcolm, takes a puff of her cigarette, and blows out a little cloud of smoke.

"Metcalf Grammar," I say.

"Where's that?" says the spiky one.

"Over towards Westbourne." I point behind me.

"So how do you know each other if you're not at the same school?" says the taller one.

"We've known each other for yonks," says Malcolm. "Our parents are friends. In fact," he pulls a big toothy grin, "our parents used to do karate together."

Everyone laughs. That is, everyone except me. It is funny, but for some reason I can't laugh.

The spiky one perches on the bench next to the tall one. "You still doing the old choppy-socky?" she asks Malcolm.

"Abso-bloody-lutely." Malcolm points to his white trousers.

"Duh," says the spiky one.

"Yeah," says the tall one. "You're looking pretty buff these days."

"Let's see your muscles, then," says the spiky one.

Malcolm leans forward, slips his jacket off one arm, and flexes his muscles. He looks like he has twisted cables under his skin, and even though his biceps look small they rise up like smooth rocks.

"Can I touch?" asks the tall one.

"Julia!" scolds the spiky one.

Julia—I think I have it now—grinds out her cigarette, shuffles along the bench towards Malcolm, then squeezes his arm while he flexes. She looks back at Julie and lets out a long whistle. "I think it's alive," she whispers.

Julie stands up and takes a seat on the opposite side of Malcolm. "Here, let me have a go," she says with her cigarette still in her mouth.

"Sorry." Malcolm slides away from Julie and maneuvers his jacket back on. Moving away from Julie brings him up against Julia—the tall one—who slides back a bit herself, but only a couple of inches. "Not for the faint-hearted."

"I'm not faint-hearted," says Julie.

"Are you on your way over to the dojo?" I ask Malcolm. He stands up. "I am, actually."

"Is that the one in Portland Road?" says Julia. "My brother used to go there."

"The very same," says Malcolm. He reaches under the bench for his gym bag.

"Oh. My place is over that way," Julia jumps to her feet. "I'll walk with you."

"Congratulations," says Julie. "When did you move?"

"Bugger off," says Julia.

"Bugger off yourself," says Julie.

Malcolm comes over and punches me on the shoulder. "Want to come along?"

"Come where?"

"Come and do a class. You can take a trial class for nothing you know. Be a blast."

"No. I've got to get back." I give him a joyless grin. "Bloody homework."

"Pain in the arse, right." He does this thumb and little finger gesture next to his head, as he walks away. "Give us a shout if you're coming over here again."

I walk to the front of the shelter and watch them head down towards Portland Road. They keep on opposite sides of the pavement. Am I reading too much into this? They're just two friends going somewhere at the same time.

There's a snort from inside the shelter. It sounds like a laugh and I look around, ready to give Julie a knowing grin, but she's sniffing snot up her nose. Suddenly she looks like a little kid, and it's weird with the grown-up hairstyle. She's slumped forward with her elbows on her knees, biting her thumbnail. "It's just you and me," I say, and modify my grin to something that I hope looks more sympathetic.

"What's that?" she says. She spits out something. Maybe a piece of thumbnail.

"I said it's just you and me."

"What's that supposed to mean?" she asks without looking at me.

"Nothing." I wish I hadn't said anything. Now it looks like I was making some kind of suggestive remark—about I don't know what—when in fact it was the last thing on my mind. I don't want to stay here with her anymore than she wants to stay here with me. I want to tell her that she looks sad, and I was just trying to make her feel better, but it all seems like it might be too complicated to explain. "Maybe I'll see you around, then," I say. I lift my bike by the saddle, put my leg over the crossbar, and rotate the pedal up so the bearings rattle.

"Maybe." She sniffs again.

"Actually, I have to use the bog before I go."

"When you gotta go, you gotta go."

I prop my bike back against the bench. "Could you watch this for me?"

"I won't take my eyes off it for a second," she says.

I go and pee. While I'm in there, I get this feeling that she's going to steal my bike, but when I come out the bike's still there. Julie's gone, though, which is actually sort of a relief, but I'm left feeling like I've just become a worse person in the last five minutes, even though I haven't done anything yet.

If Malcolm's not gay, and he's not actually cheating on Tinga with this Julia—which is what it looks like—then maybe he's not about to chuck Tinga, and I'm back up shit creek.

Not to mention I'll probably never find out why Julia's called Warty-Webster.

TEN

My guess is that Tinga's changed her routine for the night.

What's more likely is that I missed her while I was in the shelter.

I could spend all night doing loops of the park and I wouldn't see her. I might as well just cut across the middle and go home.

A narrow footpath connects to the opposite part of the park drive, which is what I ride on. A little sign says *No Cycles*, but there doesn't seem to be anyone around to stop me.

So I stand up on the pedals and cruise slowly along the footpath to get to the drive.

Just as I pass a thick hedge, the bike stops dead and I'm thrown forward onto the crossbar, which isn't much of a laugh at the best of times.

This is not the best of times, because as I pitch forward I'm nose to nose with Narrow-face. I fumble to get a better grip on the handlebars, but I just grip a big pair of hands, with really big knuckles.

"I want a word with you, sunshine," he snarls.

He really does look like his head's been crushed in a printing press. I wonder if that's what happened to him, because he's no kid. He looks older than Hugh. He looks like he might even be as old as Siggur's friend. He has stubble on his chin where he missed with the shaver.

Something about this is so pathetic it doesn't seem real. I almost want to laugh.

"Have you been hiding here the whole time?"

He seems to be alone. I wonder where his friends are. Maybe they thought the idea of hiding behind a hedge was too pathetic, even for them.

"Don't try to get clever with me."

In one quick move he lets go of the handle bars. He grips my collar in an iron fist. He pinches my skin as his big knuckles push up against my jaw, forcing my head up. He pulls the other hand back beside his face and clenches it into a fist.

It works. I'm scared. "What," I mumble, "did you want to have a word with me about?"

He twists his mouth into a snarl again. Maybe he's about to tell me, but then a dog starts barking and a really angry-sounding voice yells, "Leave him alone!"

At first I think one of the old biddies I saw earlier has come to my rescue, even though the barks sound a little deep for a Pekingese. I don't really care who the rescuer is; I'm just happy to be rescued. But my heart does a little skip as I look around to see a crimson-cheeked Tinga. Narrow-face looks around at the same moment and stumbles over my front wheel. He doesn't fall, but he loses his balance. He grabs hold of me even tighter to stop himself falling. I do a little hop and a skip, my knee gets tangled in the crossbar, and finally he lets go of me as I collapse into the hedge and roll onto the grass with the bike.

"Don't let that dog bite me," says Narrow-face, separating every word. He holds himself rigid with his arms flat to his side, like a guard standing at attention.

I notice Rosko isn't on his lead. He circles Narrow-face, and keeps barking as if he doesn't know what to do next either.

"Rosko! Quiet!" shouts Tinga. Then she wags a finger at Narrow-face. "What's he done to you?"

"You stay out of this," says Narrow-face, without taking his eyes off Rosko, but I assume he's speaking to Tinga. He looks like a soldier who's been surprised by the enemy while he's on the parade ground. "I'll see you again when you haven't got the dog." He glances back and forth between me and the dog a couple of times, then he says, "I'll be keeping an eye out for you, my friend." He nods. "I will an' all."

Narrow-face backs away, a foot at a time. Rosko keeps barking, but doesn't follow him.

I claw my way out of the hedge and disentangle myself from the bike.

Narrow-face continues to walk backwards in the direction of the playground, then turns and jogs away.

We don't say anything while we watch Rosko follow Narrow-face, barking at him a couple more times.

Finally, when Narrow-face is out of sight, Tinga straightens up and looks in my direction. She screws up her face as if she half recognizes me, but isn't sure. How bad can her eyesight be? Then she smiles.

"Hello, you."

"What'cha."

She doesn't remember my name. Why would she? Just because I've been thinking about her constantly for the last two days doesn't mean that she's been thinking about me. "Thanks," I say. I pull a branch and some leaves out of my collar. "I think I was about to get some facial rearrangement then." I hold up the branch as if it's part of the joke, and I notice my hand shaking. Why am I scared now? After it's over.

"Nah." She purses her lips. "He's all mouth and no trousers really, Jay."

I shiver when she says my name. "So you know him?"

"Sort of." She glances from side to side. "Where's Malc?"

Why is she asking me where he is? She must think I came to the park with him. "I'm on my own," I say.

"Oh. So what brings you here?"

Why am I here? *Brilliant.* The one thing I forgot to think of was a reason why I came here. I suppose I could tell her the truth and say, *I've cycled six miles just to see you.*

I can't tell her that. It would just sound sappy. What do I do? Do I lie? Dad would lie without thinking. I have to be truthful. I have to be better than he is.

I have to be.

On the other hand, if I tell her I've come all this way just to see her, then I suppose it would put her in a bit of an awkward position. The words just spill out. "I just came over to the park to see if Malcolm was here." There I go, lying again. Maybe I should change the subject. "I can't believe you actually know that skinhead."

"I don't really." She brushes her hair behind her ears. "I know him by sight. He goes to my school. His name's Colin Fawcett."

"At school? He looks about thirty."

"Yeah, he does. He looks like he should be one of the teachers, but he can't be more than seventeen."

I pick up my bike and lift it off the ground, but nothing falls off, so it's probably okay.

"I thought you were going to use some of your karate on him," I say. I point to the playground.

Ho-ho-ho. She giggles.

Something invisible grips me under the ribs.

"No. I don't think that would do any good," she says.

"But isn't that why you do it? Karate, I mean. So you can beat off attackers." I feel around my back to see if there are any more twigs.

"No, not really. I do it because I like doing it. I suppose I'm quite good at it, and I'm not much good at anything else."

"But if you wanted to, you could have really beaten him up."

"Not really." Tinga shrugs her shoulders. "I mean, if I

was a real expert, maybe. But I'm not. If he wanted to, he could have taken on me and you at the same time." She pats Rosko's head. "And the dog probably."

"But he said he was going to get you at school, when you don't have Rosko."

"No worries. Colin is far too proud to hit someone who wears these." Tinga jiggles her glasses up and down. "Plus, even he won't hit a girl, so I'm doubly safe."

I look down and notice the handlebars are askew, so I put the front wheel between my legs and the bike creaks as I straighten them up again. "You said karate was the only thing you were good at. I can't believe that."

"Well, according to my old man I'm no good at anything at all, which reminds me ..." Tinga looks over towards Marine Drive, then back towards me. "I have to go and do my homework, otherwise my mum gets really angry." She brushes her hair back from her glasses. She shrugs.

I wish she could stay longer, but I don't want to sound like a chump and she has no reason to stay here late with me. I give her the same line that Siggur gave me. "It was nice speaking with you," which sounds odd once I've said it, but Tinga doesn't pick up on my iffy English.

"Thanks. It was nice speaking to you, too," she says.

That's that. She doesn't hate me. She doesn't seem angry or freaked out that I came here to meet her, but I don't really know if she likes me enough to ditch Malcolm. She just stands there for a minute. Is she waiting for something? Is she waiting for me to hug her? I don't know. I can't look at her face, so I brush some pieces of gravel out of the grip of my bike tires. I'm a coward. I can't take that final step that might finally reveal exactly what I want to know—the very thing I came all this way to find out. I can't take that final step in case the very taking of the step makes her reject me.

The tension makes the sides of my head hurt. This is even scarier than Narrow-face.

I'm almost relieved when she turns away and yells, "Rosko!"

A few moments later, the dog appears around the corner, his ears flattened and his pink tongue dangling.

"Look at you, lovely baby," she says. She kisses him on the top of the head.

Lucky dog. He knows where he stands with Tinga. Unlike me. I wish I could go back to her house with her and sit under the kitchen table while she does her homework.

She bends down to clip his lead on. I'm thinking it's all finished, *finito, kaput,* when she looks up at me and says, "I'm heading over towards Marine Drive. How about you?"

I'm just about to say *Nah, I'm going the other way,* when I stop myself. I feel like I was just about to step off the curb looking the wrong way and a huge lorry was barreling down on me. It's not finished. Not yet anyway. I swallow what I was going to say, take a breath, and say, "Yeah. Me too." If I was heading home, I would be going in the exact opposite direction.

We turn without saying anything else, then walk towards Marine Drive. Me with my bike. Tinga with her dog. I listen to the whir of the bearings as I push the bike along beside me, and the click-click of Rosko's nails on the path. The combination sounds like some kind of clock counting down the rest of my life. Even though I really like this person next to me, I can't stop myself from fibbing to her. It's just one *porky pie* after another. Is it me? Is lying in the genes I inherited from my dad? Or is it just something about this boy-meets-girl thing? Is it like a kind of place where the rules are not quite normal? Sort of a parallel universe like you get in *Doctor Who*? In this boy-meets-girl universe, you're not just allowed to lie, it's almost expected. Is that how it works? Because if it is, then Tinga should be telling me a bunch of *porky pies*, but I don't think she is.

If it isn't some special place where lying is allowed—yet another game I'm playing for the first time and don't know the rules—then I should just come right out and reveal to her that practically everything I've told her is complete rubbish.

I'm no longer an active green belt. I didn't come here to see Malcolm. This is the wrong direction for me to go home, and that's only the start.

I look at her from the side; her hair is blowing back and she has nice small ears, unlike my monkey ears. I'd like to see her without her glasses again. I can't tell her the truth. She'd just tell me to get lost. I would if I was her.

The end of the park is only ten feet away. I can't tell her the truth, but I have to say something. She looks at me. She does the smile-frown-smile-frown thing, but this time she ends up looking gloomy, and then a wave of realization breaks over me.

Tinga doesn't know what to say to me any more than I

know what to say to her. All I have to do is say something. Anything. Why don't I just say what I want to say?

"It would be nice to see you again."

She stares at me. I've offended her. A chill runs down my legs. Is this the look she gave Narrow-face? If it is, I don't blame him for running away. She looks towards the seafront and a gust blows her hair over her face.

"It would be nice to see you again, too." She brushes her hair away from her face and gives me a smile. Right. Now she's going to brush me off, like she brushed away her hair.

"I was going to meet Malcolm tomorrow down at the pier. We were going to go on the beach. I could invite my friend Denise. If—you know—you wanted to come along, too."

Wait a minute. *Wait a minute!* I have to completely re-evaluate my entire existence. I must have misunderstood her. "Are you inviting me?"

"Yes." She looks puzzled. "That's what I was doing."

"Yeah. That would be…" I want to say *fantastic*, but it seems a little strong. "…nice."

"Are you sure?"

"Yes."

"You don't sound too sure."

"No. I'm sure."

"Brilliant." Now she gives me a full-on smile. "Bring your swimmies. It's supposed to be nice." Then, with a move so fast I don't have a second to react, she leans forward, places her hands on my shoulders, and plants a kiss just beside my mouth.

"Okay. Great. Tomorrow at the pier, then."

"Right." I hold onto the bike to stay upright.

"Come on, Rosko," she says. She takes the dog by the collar and runs across Marine Drive to the central reservation, where she stops and looks back at me.

The breeze wafts her brown hair out to the side. The sky is turning dark blue behind her, and the long line of cars heading west have their lights on. She waves.

"Bye," she shouts over the wind and the traffic.

"Bye." I turn back. I don't want to watch her walk away. I try not to form a mental image of Denise in my head as put my leg over the crossbar of my bike, because no matter how I imagine her, she's going to look totally different.

Just a minute.

"Wait!" Tinga is all the way across now. She turns and waves at me again. "What time tomorrow?"

"Two o'clock!" she shouts back.

"See you at two, then."

Some urge tells me to cross the road to her, but I ignore it, get on my bike, and ride away almost as fast I cycled away from Narrow-face. This time I give the playground a really wide berth.

It sounds terrible, but in my mind's eye I keep seeing Denise as Jacqui Davidson, the pin-up from Hugh's *Girls on Parade*.

ELEVEN

I ride my bike as close to the gates of Jubilee Pier as I can get, then I stand up on the pedals and balance on the bike while it's not moving. That way I can see over the heads of the day trippers that flow past me and crowd in through the turnstiles, like brightly dressed lemmings.

No Tinga, as far as I can see.

The pier is a big Victorian pile of wrought iron that juts out a couple of hundred yards into the ocean. It's topped with a Ferris wheel, a helter skelter, dodgem cars, and all the usual stuff that day trippers love. We locals—seagulls, we call ourselves—don't come here much. Part of the reason is that we like to think we're better than the tourists, and we like to keep our distance from them just in case anybody mistakes us for tourists. The other reason we don't go on the pier is that we already know that the rides are expensive and—not to put too fine point on it—they're crap.

I get off my bike, unbutton my shirt, put my fingers

into my armpits one at a time, then pull them out and smell them.

I hope nobody's looking. A special fragrance. Hugh's deodorant with a bass note of old armpit.

Lovely.

I'll just have to keep downwind of Denise.

I was planning to get the bus rather than bike, and I would have arrived smelling merely of deodorant, but I did this thing where I looked at the clock and thought *I've got loads of time before I have to leave.* But then by the time I'd finished prattling about, it was too late for the bus.

I suppose if I really wanted someone to blame I could blame *Mother!*

If she hadn't been out, then I wouldn't have been able to use the full-length mirror in her bedroom.

If I hadn't been able to use the mirror, then I wouldn't have thought twice about just getting back into the same clothes I'd been wearing before I did my workout with Hugh—after taking a bath, of course. I felt pretty comfortable in the baggy green T-shirt and rolled up jeans, but as soon as I saw my reflection I had second thoughts. Maybe Denise wouldn't want to fraternize with someone who looks like a garden gnome.

Next I tried the flouncy shirt *Mother!* bought me to wear to Aunt Maureen's wedding. With chino pants it looked good, but then I thought it looked a little geeky, and I have this feeling that I already look enough like a geek that I don't have to belabor the point by dressing like one as well.

Maybe I could counteract my innate geekiness with a

bit of a punk look. Black jeans, dark green shirt, and one of Hugh's denim jackets. Then it occurred to me that Tinga had seen me—and must have liked me—in my school clothes, and also in what I wore to Malcolm's, which was a tartan shirt and camouflage trousers. It would make sense that Denise would like me in the same kind of thing Tinga liked. I can't wear school stuff on the weekend, so I put the flannel shirt and camouflage pants on. They looked good, but then I worried that Tinga would think I only had one set of clothes, so I took it all off and got back into the punk stuff.

Like I said, by the time I'd gone through my personal fashion show, I was too late for the bus, so I had to ride my bike.

Just in front of the entrance to the pier is the statue of the Unknown Soldier. Grim-faced, he advances on the pier with his bayonet fixed. Like the ultimate seagull he is, the poor bugger will never reach the turnstiles of the pier. The memorial is bordered by four lampposts. I back up through the crowds and lock my bike to one of the lampposts. It's a little island of calm, as the tourists give the soldier a wide berth. Not surprising really. As Hugh once pointed out, the tourists are here for good things. He's an inconvenient reminder that all good things must come to an end, and sometimes the end can be a sticky one.

I like him though. I climb his steps, give him a hollow slap on his bronze boot for good luck, then have another look around.

After all my panic, I'm actually a few minutes early according to the old clock, although that's just a guess as it might have been reading one fifty-five for a couple of decades. I'm beginning to have my doubts about my habit of never wearing a watch. I feel like I have a sense of the time, but then I always seem to be showing up either early or late everywhere.

Now that I'm early and smelly, maybe I should just jump in the sea right now.

Too late. Here she is. Tinga's on her own with her hair swinging from side to side. She looks nice in a green suede jacket and black jeans. Too nice. Now I feel like a right scruff. I crane my neck, looking for Denise. Maybe she's coming separately.

"What'cha," I call out.

"What'cha." Tinga weaves her way between the tourists.

I'm about to come down to her, but she hops up the steps next to me.

As usual, I don't know how to start a conversation with her so I just say, "Where are the others?"

She does a sad face. "Oh. Denise isn't coming. She doesn't feel well." She has plum-colored lipstick on, and she has some of it on her teeth.

Should I tell her? Maybe not. Poor kid. She must have been as nervous about meeting Malcolm as I was about meeting Denise.

"I'm sorry." I wonder for a second if Denise maybe just didn't like the sound of me. "Nothing too serious I hope." To be honest, I'm not really sorry, but for some reason I'm still in a panic. Maybe I wasn't in a panic about meeting

Denise. Maybe I was really in a panic about meeting Tinga. Nothing to be done about it.

"Nah. Girl stuff," she says. "You know."

"Right," I say, as if I know exactly what she's talking about and it's something I come across all the time. "What about Malcolm?"

"Oh." She brushes her hair away from her face. "He said he might be late, but we shouldn't wait. He'll come and find us."

I don't know whether to be disappointed or not. For one moment I wish that Malcolm was feeling ill as well; then I stop myself, as that would be a Dad-type feeling.

"It's a bit chilly for a swim though, isn't it?" She folds her arms across her chest as if she's trying to keep warm.

She has the top button of the jacket unfastened and I could see right down inside. I could if I looked, but for some reason I have no urge to look.

"Yeah. Looks like it might rain later." In fact it looks like it could rain any minute. This could be the shortest double-date-slash-non-date in history. "Do you want to walk along the esplanade?"

"Yeah. Why not." I don't care where we go as long as I get to be with her. I jump down and we make our way through the crowd.

The esplanade is below the street level. We walk past the arcades listening to the sounds of machine-gun fire and explosions.

We walk into the noise and shadows. I'm old school when

it comes to arcade games. We play a few games at an alien-themed pinball machine, but neither of us gets replays, and we wander out in the sunshine again.

She sucks air through her teeth. "Whoa. Look at those dirty dogs."

"What?"

I follow her gaze. Down on the beach, a Dalmatian is up on the rear end of a border collie.

Ho-ho-ho. She does her laugh. I haven't heard it for almost a day, which is far too long to go without hearing it. "That's guaranteed to end in tears."

A man and a woman run towards the dogs from opposite ends of the boardwalk.

"Oscar!" shouts the woman. "Come here, you filthy dog." Oscar is not in a listening mood, so the woman drags him off by his collar and slaps him with his rolled-up leash.

"Come here, Henry," says the collie's human.

"Uh oh! Two boys!" Tinga grabs my upper arm.

Henry's owner slaps Henry's hindquarters, but not hard.

"That's not fair! What's wrong with two boys doing it if it makes them happy?" The breeze whips her hair across her face.

The first image that comes into my head is of Malcolm and me in the shower. "Are you talking about dogs or people?"

"I don't know." She turns around to make the wind blow her hair out of her face, rather than into it. "Both, I suppose."

A few brave souls are weathering the chilly afternoon and sitting out on the beach; one or two are even swimming. A mum shouts at her kids. She wraps her towel around herself in that special way that makes me think she's going to take her swimsuit off under the towel. I don't want to look but I can't take my eyes away. I actually have to cover my eyes with my hands to stop myself from gawking.

Something touches my shoulder. I open my eyes to see Tinga's hand there, with scabs on the knuckles. Somebody got punched this morning at the dojo.

"Are you alright?" she says. She tilts her head to one side and looks right into my eyes.

I think this is the first time I've actually looked straight into her eyes, and I have to swallow before I answer.

"Some sand, I think." It's a pathetic lie, as the beach is mostly rocks.

She's still staring at me, and I think this is the moment to ask a question I have to ask, but I'm not sure I want to know the answer to it. "What exactly is your relationship with Malcolm?"

She doesn't say anything right away, but she turns away and watches the Dalmatian. She probably misses Rosko. Then she looks back at me.

"Well, I've known him for about eighteen months." She brushes her hair behind her ears, but a breeze blows it straight back across her face again. "Since I've been going to the dojo."

I lean back onto the rail, haul myself up, and sit on it, facing inland.

"But we've only been going out since February." Tinga grabs hold of my arm and hauls herself up next to me. "I had been seeing this other bloke, but I was getting fed up with him. He was only interested in sex." She shuffles along the bar until I can feel the warmth of her shoulder next to mine. She puts her mouth next to my ear. "He wanted to put his penis in my mouth." She leans back. I hold my gaze on her eyes and don't look at her mouth. I don't want to imagine anything. "Don't get me wrong," she says in a normal voice. "I'm not totally against doing that. I just didn't want to do it with him."

Something about the way she says this makes me laugh. It's not funny, but I think I'm just so happy to be here, I can't stop myself. Then Tinga starts to laugh, and loses her balance. I put my hand on her back to steady her and her face comes a few inches from mine. I want to kiss her, but I think she wants to keep talking.

"Kind of surprising for a girl who wanted to be a nun."

"Wait a minute. You wanted to become a nun?"

"Yeah. I went to this place called Walsingham Abbey. Seemed like a nice way to spend your life when I was eleven. Seemed kind of magical." She grins at me. "But then I got led astray."

"By the bloke"—I'm not sure how to describe him—"you went out with before Malcolm."

"I think I probably led myself astray." She does a short laugh and almost falls right off the rail again. I put my hand on her back again to steady her. "Anyway, we decided to meet one evening to walk our dogs," she says as she tries to find her balance. "He was walking his dog in the park. We walked and talked and then he asked me to be his girl-friend." I take my hand away from her back, but she pulls it back. She tucks her shoulder into my armpit. I can smell her flowery shampoo. I hope she can't smell my armpit-deodor-ant combo. "He took me to meet his parents almost imme-diately, which was kind of weird for me because I can't take him to meet mine."

"Really?"

"Don't get the wrong idea. My parents are very nice, but they're still set on me becoming a nun. They might allow me to see a boy who was a good Catholic. Preferably one who was planning on becoming a priest."

"That doesn't really sound like Malcolm." With all this talk about Malcolm, I'm worried that when he shows up he might see me with my arm around Tinga. I'll have to make sure he realizes that it's just to stop her from falling off. And maybe a little to keep her warm. I hope he doesn't misinter-pret what we're doing. "Your parents sound a bit strict."

"My dad's Irish." She looks straight at me with her head tilted again. "He doesn't talk about it, but something hap-pened to him in Belfast during the troubles." She holds onto me tighter. "Sometimes I think he hates Protestants more than he loves Catholics. He's not that keen on the English generally."

I wave my hand towards the crowd by the pier. "There are a lot of us about."

She's quiet for a moment, then she rests her head on my shoulder. "Malcolm's parents took us out to some fancy

Italian place. I thought he was such a gentleman after the other guy."

I stare down at her straight part. My insides feel as if they're about to dissolve.

"But now, almost three months later, he hasn't done much more than kiss me on the cheek. Like this." She stretches up and brushes her lips against my cheek. "Us two. We've known each other less than twenty-four hours, and we've already gone further than I have with Malcolm."

Maybe Malcolm really is gay. Kind of makes sense if I look at it in a certain way. He doesn't want anyone to know he's gay, so he has a girlfriend to cover it up.

I think about telling her the story of the shower. Then I change my mind. It would just sound like something I was making up to drive a wedge between her and Malcolm for my own slimy purposes. Besides, I really don't care if Malcolm's gay or not. It's his business whether he wants anyone else to know.

"But you're still going out with Malcolm even if you don't really do anything," I say, which is an odd thing for me to say, because I have no idea what Malcolm should do other than kiss her. I don't know what boyfriends and girlfriends are supposed to do. I actually thought that kissing might be about the limit, but she's just told me that she isn't against the idea of putting a penis in her mouth, and there's plenty of scope for activities between that and kissing.

Does that mean she's thought about putting Malcolm's penis in her mouth?

I'm in the highly privileged position of knowing more

or less exactly what that would look like. I try not to allow what would be a very accurate image to materialize in my mind.

"Um. I don't know if Malcolm and I are much more than just friends."

And what's our relationship? I want to ask. But I don't, because it's yet another question I don't want to know the answer to, just in case it's the wrong answer.

Instead I ask her, "Do you want an ice cream?" Not so much because I want an ice cream, but because we're in front of one of those American-style ice cream places and I really want to stop talking about Malcolm. As soon as I make the suggestion for ice cream, I sort of regret it. Tinga seems so grown up. I don't know how old she is, or if she's older than me. I hope she likes ice cream. The shop says it sells thirty-six flavors, so there has to be one that she likes.

"Okay," she says, as if she's not completely sure.

I wonder for a moment if she really does think I'm childish for wanting ice cream, but then she does her laugh and takes a purse out of her shoulder bag. "My shout."

"No, you shouldn't pay for them," I say quickly.

"I want to though." She jumps down and turns to face me.

"You don't have to. Have you got enough?" I reach into my pocket. After the amusement arcade I don't have enough anyway.

"Yes." She pulls up a fiver. "To be strictly honest, it's actually my mum's shout. This is her money."

She gets her ice cream first.

She takes a big bite right away, licks the green off her lips, steps towards me, and plants a kiss right on my mouth.

I'm so shocked I just stand there. I must look a total wally with my mouth hanging open.

"Like it?" she says. I don't know if she means the kiss or the ice cream. Maybe I'm not supposed to know which one she means.

"Yes," I say, which doesn't really begin to describe what I really think, but then that's complicated, too. So I say, "You made a good choice," a statement which is also open to interpretation. "I think I'll try the blueberry."

"Yeah, why not. I like the idea of blue ice cream."

Tinga buys me a cone. I want to let her taste mine the same way she let me taste hers, but she steps back from me. Out of arm's reach. She must have learned that in karate, how to stay out of reach. So I just let her take a bite from the ice cream itself. Maybe she feels like what she did wasn't quite right.

Back on the esplanade, she stands close to me again. I think it's time to say something.

"I really like you," I say. I feel a bit of an idiot having such a serious conversation with a blue ice cream in my hand. "I really like kissing you."

"But you just want to be friends, right?"

"Well, no." I shrug. "I don't think we can be more than that if you're still going out with Malcolm."

"Okay, just one more time," she says. This time when she kisses me there's no ice cream, and the kiss feels hot and soft, and the sweetest thing I've ever done.

Then a horrible thought stabs me right in the sternum and I pull back. "Bloody hell, Tinga," I say. "What if Malcolm sees us?"

She gives me the same look she gave me at the Unknown Soldier—the uncertain grin—only this time I think I know what's going on.

"What?" I say.

"Jay, if I tell you something I did that's sort of bad, do you promise you won't be angry?"

I should tell her that it depends on what she's going to tell me, but I don't think I could ever be angry at her, so I just say, "Tell me." I think I know what she's going to tell me anyway, and I don't know how I'm going to feel about it, but I'm not going to be angry. Sad maybe. "It's okay. I won't be mad."

"Pinky promise?" She holds out her little finger like a primary-school kid.

"Pinky promise." I wrap my little finger around hers.

"Here goes," she says. "Malcolm isn't coming. I didn't tell you because I thought you might just go home, but now I suppose you probably wouldn't have."

She laughs a bit, but it's not really a merry laugh.

Talking about Malcolm doesn't make me feel like laughing at all.

"I wish you'd told me," I say. "I really don't feel what we're doing is quite right. I mean, he is still your boyfriend."

"Well, he had a grope session with Siggur. He even told me about it."

"So is this some kind of revenge?"

"*Oh bugger!* I wish I hadn't said that. It sounds all wrong. That's not what I'm trying to say."

"Well what?"

"What I'm trying to say is that Malcolm and I are history, and so it's okay."

"But does Malcolm know?"

"No. But that's not how it works. Things aren't always clear cut. It's not always like one thing finishes, then another one starts."

I don't know what to say. I'm right out of my depth. There should be some system where you can have your first boyfriend-girlfriend thing, if that's what this is, without it being all complicated. Meanwhile, my ice cream's run all over my hands, so I turn around, toss it in the garbage, and wipe my fingers on my trousers.

Then I take Tinga's ice cream and do the same, only she wipes her hands on a tissue from her shoulder bag.

She offers me a tissue, but I put my hands on her shoulders and just rest my forehead against hers. She reaches up and strokes the back of my neck, and maybe it isn't so wrong after all.

After a while we break apart and just look at each other.

I really want to see her again without her glasses. I could just reach up and take them off her, but I'm worried that if I do she'll be upset. She might think I don't like her in glasses. Or she might think I'm only interested in her because of how she looks, rather than who she is or something.

A bunch of other equally daft ideas are flitting through

my brain when, without any warning, she sticks her index fingers into my armpits.

"Hey!" I yell, and she immediately pokes me in the stomach.

I reach out to grab her, but she slips under my hands, then turns and runs. "Bit slow for a green belt, aren't you?" she says as she jumps down onto the beach and drops almost noiselessly onto the shingle.

Yes. I'm very slow for a green belt. Slower than you could imagine. I have a lot of work ahead of me. I follow her and land with a big crash that sends little rocks and stones flying.

She sets off towards the water, then turns and stops. I reach her in two giant steps, but once again she slips under my arms. I try to turn and follow, but land flat on my face in the stones. I roll over to see her red face, and feel her fingers shoved into my armpits again.

"You won't want to smell those fingers after where they've been," I yell.

She's looks like she's laughing too hard to reply. I try to get up but she pinches my waist and I fall back again.

Finally I get to my feet and she's just out of reach, bending forward with her hands on her knees. "Don't come near me or I'll throw up on you," she says.

This time I circle her like I'm stalking her.

She starts laughing and twists from left to right. Then I spring and grab her around the waist.

A second later, I'm lying half on top of her and half on the shingle.

"Gotcha," I say when I catch my breath.

I can't help it, but I'm mesmerized by the sight of her boobs rising and falling.

"What are you going to do now you've got me?"

She takes a deep breath and slides her hand around to the back of my neck, pulls me upwards so my face is level with hers, then presses her mouth against mine. My eyes close. She pushes her tongue between my lips and past my teeth. I twiddle the tip of my tongue around hers.

I open my eyes. Hers are shut tight, or at least I suppose they are. All I can see is one big shut eye surrounded by one glasses frame. She has some black on her eyelashes and something greeny-blue on her eyelid.

Then I notice I'm suffocating, so I have to pull away.

We kiss again, and then without either of us saying anything, we get up and start walking. She takes hold of my hand and swings it.

We walk towards Clifton, which is shabbier than Port Agnes and has only a smattering of day trippers. Off the channel, a squall blows in with a thunderstorm. There's a lot of yelling. There's day trippers running with newspapers held over their heads and mums ushering children into the arcades. The pensioners have seen it all before, so they tough it out with umbrellas and waterproof smocks.

There are big gaps between the flashes and the thunder. I'm usually pretty wary of thunderstorms, but I somehow feel brave. I think thunderstorms are probably really dangerous, so I don't just feel brave, I feel reckless. Like some power will protect us.

Nothing bad could happen to either of us on a day like this, so Tinga and I just keep walking and getting wetter.

We climb up to the empty bandstand, which is made of old wrought iron. My area of expertise is biology, but I've picked up a decent knowledge of physics along the way. I feel it's only fair to tell her.

"With all this iron-work around, this might not be the best place to be during a thunderstorm."

"It's beautiful though."

"It's supposed to be famous. I think it was in a film."

Rain sprays in through the open sides. Folding chairs—also metal—are arranged as if they were the ones having the party. Some of the ones in the middle are still dry.

The beach, the boardwalk, and the pavement are as deserted as if it had done a fast forward from May to November without stopping for all the other months in between.

Tinga does her shoulders-up-to-the-ears thing. "Hi," she says. She rests her forehead against my cheek. Then tips her head up and kisses me.

We sit on two of the folding chairs the band left behind and carry on kissing. Icy water from the chair soaks straight through the seat of my trousers, but I don't care. She kisses my neck, my cheek, then rests her head on my neck. I listen to her breathing.

I place my palm on her stomach. My throat feels tight as I undo two more of the buttons on her jacket. I slide my hand side to side a couple of times. My heart pounds as I slide my fingers in and upwards until I feel the lower ridge of her bra. I can hardly breathe as I slide my hand over the ridge. What

I feel then, I only feel with the edge of my index finger, and only for a second before a set of iron fingers pulls my hand out and places it outside her jacket on her stomach.

I wish I hadn't tried that move, but then she turns us around so she's on the outside. She leans forward, presses her cheek against mine, and I can see the world through her hair. Then she leans back and just smiles at me. She looks so happy. She leans forward again, but just before she blocks out my view, I see a bloke staring at us. His face is mostly hidden by his umbrella, but he looks about Dad's age and he looks angry. My first thought is that he's some religious nut, but he also looks familiar. Then Tinga starts kissing me again, and I can't really think about anything else.

Eventually the rain stops, and the sun comes out again.

"What time is it?" She leans back, looks side to side, then quickly fastens her undone buttons.

I stand on the chair. I can just see the clock at the pier. "Three-thirty."

"I'm all wet." She stands up and runs her hands down the back of her leg. "And it's all your fault."

I slide off the chair and we hug. "It's only water though."

"Duty calls." She pulls away. "Got to walk Rosko."

I want to go back to the park with her, and I could. I could just follow the bus on my bike. But she doesn't invite me, and I don't make the suggestion. Maybe we've seen each other enough for one day.

She climbs down from the bandstand, stops, and turns. Then, as if she can read my mind, she says, "I don't know if you've got the time, but I have to come into the town center again tomorrow." She shrugs. "It's supposed to be nice. Do you want to try to swim again?"

"Okay," I say. I try not to sound too keen, but I don't think I'm very convincing.

"Can you get to the Clock Tower for mid-day?" She does her frown-smile thing.

I nod slowly. "Yeah. I should be able to," I say, even though I want to jump up and down and say *Fantastic!*

"Twelve o'clock, then." She folds her lips over her teeth, and now she starts nodding as well.

We must look a very agreeable couple to anyone who's watching. "I'll be there."

She begins to walk away and then turns back. She grabs hold of my forearms and pulls them around her waist. "I'm really excited about you coming to the test."

"The test?"

"The blue-belt test!" She pushes me away, but keeps hold of my arms.

"Oh, right. I almost forgot."

"Yeah well, don't forget. I'm really looking forward to seeing you in your *gi*." She pulls me back again, then gives me a quick kiss on the lips.

"Okay."

I stay on the seat in the bandstand and watch her walk away. Even though the rain has pretty much cleared up, a little cloud comes and hovers over me. For an hour. For one amazing hour I think I knew Tinga better than I'd ever known anyone in my life. Probably knew her better than I know myself. Then in one minute—when she brought up the karate—she became a complete mystery again. Does she really like me? Or does she just like that I do karate—or, to be more precise—does she just like me because she thinks I do karate?

I know I'm being stupid. I try to shake the idea out of my head as I amble back along the beach to get my bike. I should be happy. I'm seeing Tinga tomorrow, and by that time she will have sorted out things with Malcolm. It's all going to be fine.

A shiver runs through me. What have I done? Would Malcolm and Tinga have stayed together if I hadn't come along? Even though Malcolm can be a pain, I still like him. I liked him when I was a little kid. He was a pain then as well, but he was fun to be around, and it wasn't just for the *Playboys*. He was the nearest thing I had to a best mate.

I suppose it would be too much to ask that I could have both a best mate *and* a girlfriend.

I arrive back at the Unknown Soldier. Turns out it's too much to ask to have a girlfriend and a set of wheels because somebody's pinched my bike. It's no longer chained to the lamppost. I stare at the lamppost for a few minutes as if the bike will magically reappear. Maybe the Unknown Soldier is not as lucky as I thought.

slump down on the steps of the Unknown Soldier and let the tourists flow around me.

Right now I hate happy people. In fact, right at this moment I'm not sure I even have a lot of sympathy for miserable people, not that there are any down here apart from me.

Skateboarders, grandmothers with cameras, arm-in-arm couples. As far as I'm concerned they can all take a running jump off the end of the pier.

Okay. I realize I'm overreacting. It is only a bike after all—a bike that was too small for me at that. And I don't really want to see a mass suicide. At least not the skateboarders and grandmas.

I don't really care that much about the bike. I lived quite happily without it for the last two years until last Wednesday.

The real issue is this. Without the bike I can't get to the Clock Tower tomorrow to meet Tinga, unless I go by bus, but with the way buses are on Sunday, I'll never get there by mid-day.

My relationship with Tinga is complicated enough already.

Now it's ten times more difficult.

A bloke and a girl pass me holding hands.

The bloke has shoulder-length hair and a leather jacket, even though it's warm. The girl has nicer clothes and shorter hair. When they get to the entrance of the pier, they try to go in opposite directions, but without unclasping their hands they can't get any farther apart than the combined length of their arms.

Eventually the bloke gives in and they head east. Away from the pier.

Was it difficult for them? Did the bloke have to get dressed up in armor, ride into the middle of the forest, and rescue the girl from a fire-breathing dragon? I don't think so. But if he did, he had an easier time than I'm having. At least you know where you are with fire-breathing dragons.

Thinking of dragons makes me think of the bloke who stole my bike. I have this fantasy of coming back a few minutes earlier and catching him just as he's about to ride off. He has his back to me as I slide in with a solid back kick right to his gluteus maximus. *Whoa!* he says as he goes clattering onto the pavement with the bike. The crowd of day trippers forms a circle around us as I move in.

"That's my bike!" I yell. I yank his arm up and back and lift my knee, ready to stamp my heel into his bread basket, but then he turns his head. I gasp. It's Brian Evans, the wimpiest kid in school, and he starts blubbering.

A skateboarder breaks away from the crowd. "Come on, man. He's just a little kid!"

And it's true. If anyone was puny enough for me to be able to beat them up, then they'd be so pathetic I'd have to feel sorry for him. I'd have to help him up, dust him off, and then let him take the bike to make up for scaring him.

It's far more likely that he was watching till I was occupied and out of the way. Even if he wasn't, then he was probably more like Colin Fawcett and he would have put me in the hospital.

And he'd still have my bike.

At least I'm not in the hospital.

On the other hand, he's still done me some real harm. This the first time I've been the victim of a crime. I know that it probably wasn't personal. It's not likely I knew the bloke, but I still feel like someone's actually singled me out to do me some harm. I want to tell all these people that I've been robbed. I want to wipe the smiles off their faces for a moment. Just for one moment, that's all.

It wouldn't be so bad if I'd done something to deserve having my bike stolen. I could make some sense of it then. Then I realize that maybe I have done something. I've stolen Malcolm's girlfriend. I've completely become the very thing I was trying not be. I've become the person who destroys relationships. I've become the betrayer. And it's worse. I've betrayed someone who thought I was his friend.

Whatever it takes, I have to put it right. I have to get over to Wish Park, find Tinga, and stop her before she says anything to Malcolm. If I can do that, then I can turn it all around. If only I had my bike. It's going to be a hundred times more difficult and a lot slower, but I'm going to have to take the bus.

I jump down from the monument and weave my way in between the day trippers. Once I'm off the seafront and on West Street, there aren't so many people about so I can jog towards the bus stands at Churchill Square.

Then another problem brings me back to a walk. I reach into the little corner pocket in my jeans and pull out about forty pee. Not even enough for two stops, and Wish Park is two buses and at least twenty stops. I'd need two quid at the very least. I filter the petrol fumes through my nose and shrug my shoulders to release my shirt from my sweaty back. I keep walking. At first I don't know where I'm going, but then I have an idea. Trafalgar Street isn't far. I might as well go to see if Dad's there and do my training session. He might not be there, but it's worth a try. By the time I walk home, it'll be time to leave and head out to the dojo anyway.

Then I have another thought. I'm not going to take things any further with Tinga, so there's not much point in me training any more. In fact, there are plenty of reasons for me not to train. Since my first session on Thursday, I've almost turned into a small version of Dad. Who knows how I'd end up after three weeks. But I still have to go. He's expecting me, so I have to tell him. I can't just not show up, even if that's exactly what he would do. It'll be a good deed.

Maybe if I do something good, then I'll be lucky—Tinga won't see Malcolm tonight, and I can break up with her tomorrow before she does anything.

I have to admit that making this decision leaves me feeling even more empty. I realize I was actually looking forward to the session tonight.

THIRTEEN

The dojo's locked, but the office door is open and I can see a light on.

I buzz the bell. He pokes his head around the office door, then comes out to let me in.

This would be easier if I could just tell him from the doorstep, but he doesn't give me a chance. He just says, "Come in, I'm on the phone," and jogs back to his office.

I'm going to have to go in. It seems daft to just stay outside. I bow, say "*Hooss!*" and close the door behind me, stepping into the sweaty smell of hard-working bodies.

"Look, Jason's just turned up." Dad's phone voice drifts out through the door. He doesn't whisper when he talks about me. Maybe he doesn't care. "Yes. What time's the later showing?"

He must be moving his evening plans around because he thinks I want to train now. I should just tell him. "Dad," I say as I walk towards the doorway.

"Eight o'clock. That'll be perfect." He pokes his head around the door. "Just a minute, Jay."

I wave my hand and then mouth *I'm not going to train now*, but he's turned his back and doesn't see me.

I go right up to the door and peer around the gap.

He has his back to me with the phone up to his ear. He's tapping the computer keyboard, but I can hear an angry squawk from the phone earpiece.

"Look. I'm really sorry," he says.

Who's he talking to? He didn't say *my son, Jason* he just said *Jason*. Whoever he's talking to knows me. Or at least knows *about* me.

"Dad," I whisper.

He takes his hand off the computer keyboard and waves me away from the door.

And the word is there in my head. *Girlfriend.* He's talking to his girlfriend. I shake my head. This is all wrong. I think about when I was talking to Siggur. I'm living in this little protective cocoon, and she's right. It's time for me to come out of it and find out things for myself.

"I said I'm sorry, but you knew this was something that was going to happen …"

The phone squawks angrily.

This is useless. I don't want to listen to his conversation anyway. I turn around and shuffle back out into the dojo proper. There are no seats, but there's a broad ledge under the front window, so I sit on that.

The door opens after a few moments. I stand up. I have my speech all ready, but he bursts out with a large white package in his hand. I open my mouth, but before I can get a single word out he shoves the package at me.

"I'm just going to be a few more minutes on the phone," he says. "Is white okay? I couldn't get black in your size."

I stare down at the package in my hands. A clear plastic cover. A white jacket. He's got me a set of *gi*.

I can't tell him now.

"Go and try them on." He grins at me and points to a door with *Boys* painted on it.

"Thanks," I mumble. I say it to his back as he returns to the office, and this time he shuts the door behind him. I can still hear his voice.

"I'll get there early and buy the tickets," he pleads into the phone. "I'll meet you outside."

I stand there for a minute. I don't know what I'm waiting for. His conversation isn't going to end any time soon.

I look down at the brand new *gi*. Whiter than they'll ever be again. I was assuming I would just have to dig up my old uniform and scrub the mold off it. Not to mention taking into account how much I've grown in the last two years—a little up, and more than a bit sideways—it's probably going to be tighter than a straitjacket. Come to think of it, right now a straitjacket might be more suitable for me than a karate uniform.

"You know what you mean to me," he says into the phone. He's using his karate skills to make everything okay with his girlfriend, and he's good at it. He's really good. Oh yeah. Comes from years of training. He knows exactly when to let his opponent make the moves; he knows when to dodge to the side, he knows what to deflect, and he knows how to seize the moment and strike back.

And he strikes back hard.

I don't want to hear any more. I don't want to learn anything here, but if I did, it would be how to punch and kick. I don't want to learn how to make people do things they don't want to do. I jog across the dojo to the changing room. With the door shut tight behind me, I can't hear any more of the conversation.

When I come out, he's in the middle of the floor with his hands behind his back.

"Now you look the part," he says. "A perfect fit."

I check out my reflection in the long mirror.

"The trousers are a bit long." I hitch them up at the waist, but they slump down over my feet as soon as I take my hands away.

"Maybe this'll help." He steps between me and the mirror and produces a green belt.

It glows in the neon light. I have to swallow.

He pulls it taught so it makes a snapping sound, swings it over my head like a jump rope, then knots it around my waist.

"Now we're in business."

I don't want to look, but I can't help it. With the belt pulling around my waist, my trouser bottoms are now an inch above my feet.

He grins at my reflection. I look back at his, but I refuse to smile. I bite my lip.

Maybe I'm not a ninja warrior, but I'm not quite the same Jay I was five minutes ago.

How did he know—because I can't believe that he didn't know—that I had come down here to tell him I didn't want to train anymore?

I turn to face him. He bows and shoves a jump rope into my hands.

"Three minutes," he says.

The session goes much the same as Thursday's, except the warm-up is easier.

After one round with the jump rope, the stiffness is gone. To be honest, I'd forgotten about it until it was gone. Like one of those annoying noises you only notice after it stops.

This time we work through some drills. I do some side kicks, some punches, and then we try the thing I hate most which is the jump back kick. He's always encouraging and never sarcy. The last jump back kick even knocks him off balance, although I have a feeling he stumbled on purpose to make me feel good. Then we spar. This time he brings out a different tote. He tips out pink-and-white armor.

"Sorry. It's the girls', but you can use the white."

I really have to hold back a smile when I think about how girls are so attached to pink that they even use it for beating each other up.

I wonder if Tinga has pink armor.

I get the sequence right this time. Gloves on last, otherwise you can't fasten the straps.

I roll forward onto my feet in one movement, and turn to check out my reflection.

A chill runs through me, all the way from my feet to my neck.

The figure staring back at me from the mirror with the white *gi*, white shin guards, white gloves, and white head gear is a mini storm trooper.

I haven't become *like* my dad. I have become him, or at least a small version.

I've become the very last thing I wanted to become.

I want to take the armor off, throw it on the ground, and leave.

"Come on, Jay," says Dad. "You have to keep moving or you'll stiffen up."

I shuffle around to face him. I don't know what to do. I really need someone I can ask. For now I'll have to go through the motions.

I bow and crouch into my stance, but then I just stand there.

I expect Dad to move off to the side, but he just stands there, too. He doesn't even get into a stance with his fists protecting his face, but just rests his fingers on the tops of his legs.

Moments trickle by and nothing happens.

I know I can't win, so why do anything? I don't keep completely still. I shift the weight gradually from my front to my back foot. Is the move too small for him to notice? I don't know. This time I look right in his eyes for as long as I can. I can't hold his stare, but this time when I look away, I don't look down. Instead I look up. From where I'm standing, the top of his head lines up with the ridge where the wall meets the ceiling.

Concentrate!

Then his head drops.

No conscious thought passes through my mind. My feet jump and my hips spin backwards on their own.

As I turn my head, something pink and knobby whooshes in front of my face. A second later, my foot flies out and thuds into his underarm.

I land back on one foot just in time to see his right hip flick forward.

I take a long step back. This time his foot flies past my face. I bat it out of the way and throw another back kick. This one is more of a push. It catches him in his side, just below his ribs, and the unthinkable happens. He stumbles. He only falls back a foot, and only for a second. But he stumbles. Then the unthinkable is followed by the inevitable. He fakes a punch, then slaps me on the back of the head. He pushes me back with a side kick right to the stomach. I try one more back kick, but my foot misses him by a yard and I turn right into his roundhouse, which whacks me across my shoulders.

Then the kicks start landing on me from every direction. It's like he has a dozen legs. A second later, I'm backed right into the corner between the front window and the mirror with my hands covering my face.

There's a pause in the kicks, but I keep my hands up. Never trust a sparring partner, especially if he's your dad.

First I have to point out that not one of the kicks hurt. They weren't meant to. But I never realized how much I like breathing.

I want to do more of it. Much, much more. I drop my hands and lean forward with my hands on my knees and gulp down great drafts of air.

"You little rascal."

I look up and my heart skips a beat. He's blowing air as well. Not as much as me, but he's still puffing, and his forehead is shiny.

"I taught you well." He grins at me, steps forward, and this time I can't resist giving him the smallest smile as he pulls me into his sweaty chest.

He pushes me away, pulls off my head gear, and tousles my hair. "Let's go and try that Indian. I don't know about you, but I'm famished."

"I think I'll throw up if I eat a curry." I unfasten the gloves and throw them on the floor.

"Five minutes time and you'll be starving."

FOURTEEN

Back in the changing room, I strip off my *gi* and get back into the punk gear I had on before. I'm glad I have the *gi*. They're soaked and I would have been cold and uncomfortable on the way home if I'd poured that amount of sweat into my shirt and jeans.

I tell Dad I don't want to take the uniform home. I don't want to have to hide it from *Mother!* and I don't want to have to explain why I have it. He takes it back to his office, along with the belt, and hangs them up so they'll be dry and mold-free for tomorrow.

We walk in silence till we reach West Street. Then he says, "Look. I'm not prying, and you don't have to tell me anything you don't want to, but it might help us both if you just told me a little about what brought on this sudden urge to train again."

I don't know how to begin without telling him everything.

"I mean," he says, "I'm assuming this urge didn't just come out of the blue."

We start to pass lighted shop fronts as we get nearer to the Clock Tower. In front of a bike shop, he takes hold of my shoulder to stop me, then turns me to face him. "Jay. I'm sorry if I'm barking up the wrong tree, but I have seen things like this before." He folds his arms, and looks away for a moment. I know it's hard for him to talk to me about anything important, and I know he wants to now. "Jay. Has someone threatened you?"

I shrug.

"If so, I would advise you to deal with this threat in a non-physical way if you can."

"No. Nobody's threatened to beat me up if that's what you mean."

I can't suppress a tiny smile as I think of adding... *apart from Hugh, of course*, but that would make Dad laugh, and I'm not here for his amusement.

"Don't get me wrong. Your sparring skills are very good. For a green belt who hasn't trained for two years, they're amazing. But sparring is very different than fighting."

"That's not why I want to train."

"Aha. So there is a specific reason for this change of heart."

That was sly. Yes, now I remember. He has a way of getting information. "Okay. Yes, there is."

"Like I said. You don't have to go into details, but let me ask you one more question." He wags a fat but perfectly manicured finger at me. "Are you just doing this to get into shape?"

"No. I need to work on my karate skills."

He starts walking again, but then stops almost immediately. "You're being very mysterious, Jay."

I take a long breath. "You said you wouldn't pry."

"No, no, *no*. I'm not prying. Because you've given me such a short time frame, it would help if I had at least a vague idea of what you want to achieve." Now he points his finger at me. "For instance, if you were determined to fight someone, and I couldn't persuade you otherwise, I would focus on making you strong and fast with a few simple boxing moves." He crouches down and shuffles towards me, throwing punches at the air in front of my face. "If you just wanted to get into shape, I'd focus on your cardio." He pats his chest. "Another scenario might require that you just look really good. In that case I would work on your form so that you could develop some graceful and impressive kicks rather than the bone-breakers you might need for defense."

"Why would I want that?"

"Well, if there was another person who was spurring you back into training again, and that person wasn't so much an enemy as—say—a friend." He opens his eyes really wide and grins. "Perhaps this person might even be a girl."

"You said you wouldn't pry!"

The street, the shops. Everything goes out of focus except Dad's face. Before I can tell him it's none of his business, he throws a hook punch at each of my shoulders and slaps the top of my head. "Jay, you scallywag. I can't think of a better reason to take up training again. I'm going to turn you into an artist. By the time I'm through with you, she'll be putty in your hands. You'll float like a butterfly and sting like—well, maybe not a bee, but maybe—a sand fly."

He guffaws.

"I can't believe you think this is funny! This is my life you're making a joke out of. Haven't you done enough damage to me?"

"Whoa! Steady on. I'm not laughing at you. I'm laughing because I'm just so relieved that you have a girlfriend."

Wait a minute. *Relieved?* Why relieved and not proud? "Why?" I almost can't get the word out. It's not so much that it's a question I don't want to ask. It's also a question I don't really want to know the answer to.

"*Why?*" He stops laughing. In fact he stops smiling. "Because…" He shrugs. "Because it means you're turning out alright."

"*Alright!?*" Now I try to grab his shoulders, but my hands are too small to get a real grip. "What exactly do you mean?"

"That you're normal."

I get it. "You mean that I'm not a queer."

He squeezes his nose. "If you want to put it like that." He lets out a long breath. "There was a time I was really worried you were going to turn out to be a wooftah like Malcolm Briscoe."

I want to shout, but my voice actually comes out quite soft. "So what if Malcolm's gay? What harm has he done to you? You want to know the whole story. You do. I know you do. I met a girl. Like an idiot I told her I was a green belt, so she invited me to take part in her blue-belt test. I think she really likes me…"

My father snorts.

I'm not finished. "Look. Do you think you were my first choice of trainer? Do you think I wanted to come to you? Let me tell you I tried virtually every other karate practitioner in Port Agnes-on-Sea before I came to you. I kid you not. If there had been a lame, one-legged, yellow-belt novice available, I wouldn't have come to you. You were my last resort."

My dad holds up his hands as if I've been hurling punches at him.

"Okay. *Okay!* If we're going to hurl wild accusations around, let's do it over a chicken tandoori. But let me just tell you one thing. You say you don't care if Malcolm's queer, and you're entitled to your views, but the whole reason I broke away from the Briscoes is because Malcolm tried to do something very disgusting to Hugh."

My insides knot. I shake my head.

"Hugh wouldn't make it up." Dad—of course—misunderstands why I'm shaking my head.

I look down at my feet. He's doing to me exactly what he was just doing to his girlfriend—or whoever it was on the phone when I came down to the dojo. He's using his karate skills to make me do what he wants me to do. To make me think what he wants me to think. It's just that now that we're out of the dojo, he's throwing ideas instead of punches, rumors instead of kicks, and he's dodging and weaving whenever I throw anything back.

"It happened in their shower out by the pool."

I keep shaking my head.

"I'm sorry, Jay, but some things are just wrong in my opinion. Look, let's have something to eat, then sleep on it." He spreads his arms and for one moment I think he's going to hug me again. "We can live with our differences. Tomorrow we'll start serious training."

"No." This isn't working. None of it is working. I'm sorry he bought me the new *gi*, but I have to finish what I came here to do today. All I wanted from Dad was karate training. That's all. I don't want anything else from him, but he doesn't get it. He thinks I want him to be a dad again. He probably thinks I need his decisive manly influence, or some crap like that. I don't want him getting involved in my life again. I don't want him interfering and trying to make decisions for me. I know exactly what's going to happen if I keep seeing him. Two or three more training sessions and I'm going to be living my entire life just the way he wants me to. "No."

"What do you mean *no*?" He chuckles, but it's not a confident chuckle.

I really have caught him off guard. He doesn't know what I'm going to do next, and I have to follow through.

"No!" I shuffle my feet backwards. In the direction of home.

"Jay, don't." He takes a couple of steps towards me and grabs my arm. "Jay. Is this really about Malcolm, or is it about what you think went on with your mother and me?"

I don't say anything. I swing my arm around to break his hold. I still have the upper hand.

"Jay." He puts his arms behind his back. "It wasn't all my fault. You know that, don't you?" He sounds pleading, and it makes me hate him even more.

I keep walking.

"Jay, your mother wasn't exactly a saint, you know."

His voice cuts through the night air, but it's too weak and far away to have any effect on me now. "Jay. Don't be so hasty."

Pathetic.

I turn my back and walk more quickly. Unbelievable. I've done it. I really have. I've got away clean. It's beginning to get cold. My pace warms me, and as it warms me I start to pull it all apart. Was that true about Malcolm and Hugh? It would have to be. It would be too weird for Dad to pull that out of nowhere, when it's almost exactly what happened to me.

If it is true, then is Malcolm really gay?

If Malcolm's tried it on Hugh and me, then who else has he tried it on?

And if he is gay, then what does that mean for Tinga and me?

What the heck! A speeding car almost flattens me as I try to cross Westbourne Street. I was looking the wrong way.

I haven't got away from Dad at all.

What he just told me is going to influence my next big decision.

Unless I don't let it.

It's like one of those courtroom dramas where the witness is unreliable.

Inadmissible evidence.

FIFTEEN

It's almost seven by the time I get home. Hugh is watching the football results, and he has that glazed look he has when he's watching TV. "Manchester United, two; Liverpool, nil. Newcastle, one; Tottenham Hotspur, one..." chants the announcer. I crash down next to Hugh and watch. I'm not especially interested in football, but I like watching the results. It's a simple world. The better team wins and nothing can change that. It's not just the results of a bunch of games; it's the end result of a week where everything makes perfect sense. For a few minutes I can forget real life where nothing makes sense. In real life, the person who plays a better game can just as easily win as lose. Or think he's won when he's actually lost.

Then the phone rings. Hugh slaps my leg. "You want to get it?"

"Why? *Mother!* can get it. Probably for her anyway."

"Nah," says Hugh. He has his glazed look back. "Someone rang for you about an hour ago."

"For me?" My heart actually races.

Tinga.

It has to be her. Who else would ring me? How would she get my number? From Malcolm perhaps. Then I get it—she wants to cancel tomorrow.

"*Mother!*'s up in the attic anyway," says Hugh.

I suppose I have to face the music. In a couple of swift moves, I'm out in the hall with the phone clamped to my ear. "Yeah. Hello."

Nothing. I half put it back then give it another try. "Who is it?"

"Jay. It's Malcolm."

"What'cha, Malcolm!" I'm so relieved it's not Tinga, but only for a second, because as soon as I stop worrying that it might be Tinga I start wondering why Malcolm's calling me on a Saturday night. As soon as I start wondering, I sort of know. I have no idea what to say so I just press the receiver to my ear and listen to someone talking loudly in the background. They must be watching another TV channel.

I'm just about to say something inane, like *It's a nice day*, when he solves the problem for me and says, "Guess what just happened to me today."

When he says that, I know for certain. The actual words he used were, *Guess what happened to me today*, but he said them as if he was saying, *Some friend you turned out to be, you bloody wanker.*

Like any drowning man, if I see a straw I'll make a grab

for it. Maybe I'm just imagining the accusation in his voice. Maybe he's ticked off about something else entirely. I try to make a joke. "I dunno. You're getting married."

There's a pause just long enough for me to swear to myself that I should never, ever try to be funny again.

"Ha ha," says Malcolm. This is not a laugh. He literally says *Ha, ha.* "You couldn't be more wrong. Tinga just gave me the big 'E' this afternoon."

Even though I knew exactly what he was going to say, when he actually tells me, it's like a slap. Or even a punch. Maybe the shock has something to do with the fact that he really does sound brassed off, and the entire time I've known him, which is nearly my whole life, I don't think I've ever heard him sound mean or angry. At least not as much as he does now.

Up until a few minutes ago, if you had asked me to describe Malcolm in one word, I would have said he was chirpy. In fact, I've always thought of him as being over-friendly, and I think I sort of even despised him a little for it.

So Tinga must have got to the park at her usual time, Malcolm must have been right there, and she must have given him the push.

"I'm sorry, Malc." I shrug, which is a useless gesture as he can't see me. I really am sorry but I can't begin to tell him why.

"Yeah. Me too." He lets out a long breath. "Can you believe it?"

He says this like a little lost kid who's run away from home. The tension drains out. He really doesn't know it's me, but with the tension gone, something else rushes in to fill the empty space. Something dark and sour. It takes a second for me to put a name to the feeling. Then I get it—regret.

Regret has its own voice. *If only...* it says. I start to babble to drown out the voice.

"On the other hand, you did say you weren't that interested in her anymore," I say, and then immediately wish I hadn't. I should be trying to make him feel better, not making him feel like it was probably his fault.

"Nah." Someone's really shouting in the background now. Sounds like they're watching some kind of action flick. "I would never have said anything like that."

Regret keeps washing over me. This is my chance to be a better person. I should just tell him everything.

No. I have to do better than that. I have to put it right again. I have to break up with Tinga and try to make her go back to him. Yes. I can do that. I wish I could just ring her up and do it now.

"What makes it worse is that she cheated on me," he says.

"Women. Right," I say, like I'm a veteran of dozens of failed love affairs. I think I have both feet entirely in my mouth at this point. Not only do I have no clue what I'm talking about, but Malcolm knows better than almost anyone that I have no idea what I'm talking about.

"No. I don't blame Tinga," he says.

"I suppose not," I say, but I don't think I'm really focused.

Maybe I'm trying to listen to the yelling in the background, because the next thing he says almost knocks me over.

He says, "I think someone pushed her into it. Someone with no conscience smooth-talked her into it."

It's like one of those knockout kicks that get hidden behind a fake kick.

There's a tear in the wallpaper. Just a tiny one, but I get my fingernail underneath the paper and pull. The paper opens out into a gash. Like skin being pulled back. "Sounds like a real bastard."

"You're telling me," he says, and when he says it, I wonder again if he knows the bastard is me.

I pull back more of the paper. "Maybe it'll work itself out," I tell him. At least this is honest. I hope it will work itself out, because I'm going to do my level best to put it right.

"Do you know who it is?"

"Nah," he says. "Got to be someone who goes to the park though."

The shouting in the background gets louder. They should turn the telly down. Then the person shouting yells, "Malcolm get off the phone, we're going over there right now!"

Holy crap. It must be his dad. I thought mine was bad.

"Listen, I've got to go," he says. "I don't want to say who I think it is right now, but when I meet this berk, this wanker, this arsehole, I have some really special moves for him. He's going to be really sorry."

The phone clicks off. I just stand there. "I'll keep that in mind," I say into the dead line, and it's a shame he's hung up, because it's probably the only intelligent thing I said in the whole conversation. My hand begins to ache with the weight of the receiver, so I place it back on its cradle, and pull back a little more of the wallpaper. I can hardly think about this; it makes me feel awful. I'm not scared that Malcolm's going to beat me up. I'm not saying that he couldn't. I'm saying that I don't think it's the kind of thing he'd do, especially not to me, and especially not now that he's about a foot taller than me.

No, I don't feel bad out of fear. I just feel awful guilt. The poor bloke gets dumped by his girlfriend, and then without a beat, his old man flies off the handle about something else that sounds like he's being blamed for.

I could have stopped Tinga from breaking up with him. If I hadn't sat around feeling sorry for myself at the Unknown Soldier, I would have been able to get the bus right away, and probably got to the park. If we hadn't played stupid arcade games, I would have had enough money for the fare. I can't believe how crap these things turn out.

"Jason." *Mother!*'s voice makes me jump. It's like I've been asleep for hours and she's woken me up. I turn around, and she's at the top of the stairs. Was she listening? After listening to the conversation in Dad's office, I wouldn't be surprised if she could not only hear every word Malcolm said, but probably his old man yelling, too.

"What on earth are you doing?" She's wearing dirty jeans and a T-shirt, and a big pair of yellow gloves are covering up all her bracelets and rings. At her feet is an old suit-case. "Have you finished on the phone?"

"Oh. Yeah, Mum—I mean *Mother!*" I feel like I need to give her an explanation for just standing there for no reason. "I was thinking." This is true, but it's not the truth, and what is the truth? Dad betrayed his marriage vows. That's true, but is it the truth? Just because he's a proven liar doesn't mean that every single thing he says is a lie. *Your mother wasn't exactly a saint.* That's what he said.

"Thinking is good. Who was that on the phone?"

"Malcolm Briscoe." I use both names to distinguish him from all the other Malcolms I know.

"Ah, that's nice of him to ring you. I hope you two become friends because he is a very considerate young man."

"Yes," I say, and grit my teeth.

Not exactly a saint. It's like a puzzle where you're trapped in a room with two doors. One door leads to hell and one to heaven. In front of each door is a guard. One guard always tells the truth and one guard always lies, but you don't know which guard is in front of which door and you only have one question. I wish I knew what that question was.

Mother! doesn't say anything for a moment, and I think she wants me to agree more fully with what she's said, but I can't really think of anything more to say on the subject.

"Well, I've been cleaning up," she says finally, "so I need a cigarette and a coffee."

"Okay." I look down at the case.

She follows my gaze. "These are some of your father's

things. I was hoping one of you strong boys would take it over to Granny Smallfield's."

"I would…" For once I have a real excuse. "…but I have to see someone tomorrow at the Clock Tower."

"Well, that's perfect. Granny Smallfield is only ten minutes up from there. Do you think you could take it?"

I can't think of a good reason why I can't take the case. At least I can't think of a reason I want to tell *Mother!* I mean, I'm meeting Tinga for the last time ever. I shouldn't have to carry my dad's old baggage on any date, least of all the last one. Besides, I'll have to leave three hours early if I'm going to walk and carry a heavy case.

A little light bulb comes on in my head. "I'll take it to Granny Smallfield's, but can you make Hugh give me a lift to the Clock Tower?"

SIXTEEN

I'm squashed on the back of Hugh's red-and-black Kawasaki as we hurtle along West Street through the narrow gaps between buses, taxis, trucks, and kamikaze pedestrians.

"Relax and go with the flow," Hugh said back at the house as he helped me strap the helmet on.

I think I misunderstood what he meant by *flow*. Hugh likes to ride hard, which is not exactly relaxing for his passengers. And his riding style really could initiate a certain kind of flow, but the less said about that the better. When he accelerates, I'm thrown back against Dad's old suitcase that's strapped to the rear carrier. The handle digs into the middle of my back. After a few moments of hard acceleration, Hugh has to slam on the brakes to avoid hitting whatever is in front of us, and I'm thrown forward so my crash helmet bangs against the back of Hugh's helmet.

Hugh turns around, almost facing me. "Are you frightened of bears?" he yells. At least I think that's what he yells.

His voice is muffled by his visor, and almost drowned out by the roar of the bike.

"What bears?" I squeeze my eyes shut as we seem to be about to smash into the back of a box van.

"I said are you alright back there?"

I nod, and my helmet clacks against his yet again.

Hugh has to turn quickly back to the front. An emergency has arisen. Our speed through the crowded shopping district has dropped below sixty. Hugh opens the throttle. The vibrations churn my stomach and once again I'm thrown back against Dad's case.

I'm sure the front wheel comes off the ground.

Hugh flips up his visor as we approach the Clock Tower. "Is he there?"

I told Hugh I was meeting a friend at the Clock Tower, so he naturally assumes that the friend is a bloke.

"She," I yell. Tinga's staring up North Road, which is probably the direction I'd be coming from if I was on my bike. "And yes, she's there."

She glances right at us, but she isn't expecting me to turn up on the motorbike and doesn't recognize me.

When Hugh is fully kitted out, he looks like some kind of sci-fi knight errant in his black oil-skin jacket, black helmet, and black jeans. The Black Knight of Port Agnes.

In his spare helmet and anorak, I probably look like the Black Knight's sidekick: the Lime-green, Florescent-orange Knight. My quest is to rescue a damsel-in-distress from myself.

I wasn't sure I wanted Hugh to know anything about

Tinga, but now that the moment is here, I feel a surge of pride.

"Fancy," says Hugh. I catch sight of his face in the wing mirror just in time to see him roll his eyes.

It would be all too easy to relax and go with the flow.

Hugh leans the machine so far over my knee almost brushes the asphalt. The bike pops and backfires as it slows down, and Hugh heads for the curb and plants his boot to keep the bike upright.

"Thanks," I say. I unhook my hand from the saddle-strap and flex the life back into my fingers. Then I realize that since I'm sandwiched between Hugh's back and the suitcase, I can't figure out how to get off the thing.

"Alright then," says Hugh, with a hint of impatience.

"I'm stuck."

"Put your hands on my shoulders and push yourself up!" yells Hugh.

I realize my mistake. I glance behind me to where I last saw Tinga.

She's staring at me with her hand over her mouth. She's impressed that I'm on a motorbike. This is not going to make things any easier.

There's nowhere to put the helmet, so I plant it back on my head. I push up on Hugh's shoulders and swing my leg back over the saddle, but my foot catches on the carrying rack and I sprawl across the pavement. I lie there for a second on the cold concrete and watch the passing feet of the bargain hunters stepping around me.

Hugh caves in and switches off the engine. He puts

the bike on its stand with the exaggerated patience of the extremely irritated.

I roll up into a sitting position and slip off the helmet as Hugh drops the suitcase onto the pavement next to me.

Tinga jogs across West Street towards us.

"Don't mention it," says Hugh.

"Thanks, Hugh," I say. I can't take my eyes off her.

"Hiya," she says, a little out of breath.

I don't know much about etiquette, but I think it's supposed to be rude to stay sitting on the pavement while a girl is speaking to you, so I pull myself onto my feet, which is not easy, as my legs are still vibrating.

Tinga swings her bag over her shoulder, puts her hands on my arms, and plants her sweet, soft mouth on the corner of mine. Right in front of my brother.

"This is Hugh," I say. "My big brother."

"Hi, Hugh."

Hugh puts out a large, black-gloved hand. Tinga places a small pink hand in it.

"I'm Tinga."

"What'cha, Tinga." Hugh looks her straight in the eye, but drops his gaze to her chest level for half a second, then says, "I'll leave you two to it."

He jumps back on the bike and starts it in a single movement, then banks steeply into a U-turn and roars back up West Street towards the station.

"Bloody show-off," I say to the back of Tinga's head as she watches him disappear over the brow of the hill.

"Let's go for a dip then," she says as she tilts her head in the direction of the seafront. She looks at the case and grins. "Are you off on your holidays right away?"

"Holidays? In my dreams. It's some of my dad's stuff." I'm about to kick the suitcase, as if I don't care about it, but then I stop myself and just tap it with my foot. "My mum found it in the basement." I have this idea that even the most casual friends can tell I'm a product of a broken marriage, so I watch her face for some kind of reaction, but it doesn't have any effect. I spell it out. "My parents are divorced. My mother keeps finding my dad's stuff when she does her spring cleaning, which she seems to do about once or twice a month all year round, and it's usually either me or Hugh who has to take it back."

I drag the suitcase closer. Not so much because I'm scared it'll be stolen, but because the crowd of tourists is thickening like gravy and I don't want it to be kicked over.

"I'm sorry." She turns her head so her hair swings out, exposing her sticky-out ears. The sight of them makes my heart flutter. "Actually, Malcolm told me about your parents."

A heavyset man with an ice cream bumps her and she falls against me. I get a waft of her flowery smell again. This is going to be harder than I expected.

"Can we move on?" she asks. "I think I'm going to get into a fight if we stay here."

"No problem." I take a firm grasp on the handle. The case is just a little too heavy to carry normally, so I heft it onto my shoulder like some jungle porter in an old Tarzan movie.

"I can help you with that if you like."

"No. It's not heavy, it's just the handle is about to come off." Can't I be honest about anything? How much would it hurt to tell her that I would feel embarrassed if she was carrying the case. "Let's go towards Black Rock. It'll be less crowded."

I head even farther away from my final destination, weighed down with the burden of the remnants of You-Know-Who's marriage to *Mother!* I use one hand to steady the case on my shoulder. Tinga goes around to the other side, and I feel her warm fingers grip my free hand.

"Look, Tinga."

She squeezes my palm.

A little charge runs up my ulna, but I force myself not to squeeze back. "I don't know if we should really be doing this."

"What, swimming together?" She smirks at me as we stop in front of the McDonald's at the bottom of Ship Street.

"Well, maybe that, but I meant going out together."

"Hoooooowhat!?" She turns towards me so fast I think she's going to roundhouse kick me.

"It's not about you, or anything you've done," I say. I relax my hand, and she lets go. "Or not done."

"So what is it then?" She shoves her hands into her jacket pockets.

A gap opens up in the traffic. "Let's cross here." I resist the urge to hold her hand across the street. "I know it sounds daft, but I feel a complete bastard for two-timing Malcolm."

"No. It doesn't sound daft. But it's me who was two-timing Malcolm. Not you."

We get halfway across, then have to stop at the center island to let a police car go by.

"Tough titties," she says. "He'll get over it. Shit happens."

"Malcolm rang me yesterday evening," I say. "He's really browned off and that's putting it mildly." I take a gander at our reflection as we pass a souvenir shop window. We look a sight. Me with the case on my shoulder, Tinga with her chin tucked into her collar. Tinga looks almost as tall as me. Maybe I'm shrinking.

"But that doesn't make any sense," she says. "I saw him yesterday at the park, and I told him I didn't want to see him again. He seemed fine with it. He said he'd been thinking about it himself. He thought it was a good idea. In the end, he almost made it sound like it was a mutual decision."

"Well, he's pissed off now." My shoulder is killing me, so I drop the case and heft it onto the other shoulder. I look at Tinga and she looks away. Is she telling me everything?

We clump down the stone steps to the beach. "By the way, did you tell him you were chucking him for me?" I ask as I jump off the last step and sink into the shingle with the extra weight of the case.

Tinga squats down to pick up a shell. "No. He asked me if I was going out with anyone else." She throws the shell away. "I told him I was, and he didn't seem to care. He even said *good luck*."

The tide's out, which means the beach is wide and the crowd is spread out. We'll probably be able to get a bit of privacy, which we're going to need.

"Anyhow, come on, Jay. This is the real world. People get dumped. Relationships end." She reaches up and taps the case. "Let me take it for a bit."

I hand her the case and she hugs it to her chest. We crunch over the rocks to the breakwater.

"Crikey. What have you got in here?"

"Building materials."

"You what!"

"Actually, I have no idea."

We walk in silence for a minute, then she says, "I expect Malcolm must have been putting a brave face on it." She lowers the case onto the shingle and rolls her shoulders. "Maybe he was all cut up, but didn't want to show it. Either that or he mulled it over and changed his mind afterwards."

I carry the case the last few yards to the breakwater, then I drop it. Tinga sweeps her hair behind her ears and looks me up and down.

"Where are your swimmies?"

"I've got them on underneath."

"Well, me too, but where's your towel?"

I shrug. "I don't know. I'll dry off in the sun. The case was enough to carry without having to carry a towel as well."

"We can share mine." She spreads her towel out and we strip down to our swimsuits. All I notice is that she's wearing a one-piece because I look everywhere except at her, which is strange because if I didn't know her and I was watching from a distance, I'd be assessing every one of her physical features.

"Can I ask you a personal question?" she says.

I shrug.

"How many girlfriends have you had before me?"

"One or two," I say without really thinking. "Let's go in." We pick our way over the sharp rocks towards the water.

"One or two?" She turns her foot and places it on a smooth rock.

"Well, one." Can I count my cousin Jennifer as a girlfriend? "None actually."

"Really? I suppose I ought to have guessed, but it seemed like, I don't know, hard to fathom."

"I know."

We reach the edge of the water. Tinga picks up a strip of seaweed with her toes, then flicks it at me. No sign of a smile though. "Jay. You don't have to do this. Malcolm will be fine in a week or two. He'll find someone else pretty quick if he wants to." She wades in up to her knees, then turns back towards me. "I don't want to break up with you. I like you. I think you're sweet and funny."

"I like you too, but why can't we just be friends? I mean, just for now anyway."

"Leave it out. We've come too far to be just friends. Aside from which, you have a really sweet mouth and I like kissing you." She leans towards me and brushes her lips against mine. "I can't be friends with you. I'm going to want to kiss you every time I see you."

We wade farther into the waves. I scoop the chilly water over me to get used to it.

"Listen Jay, are you holding out on me? This isn't some

elaborate ruse is it? You're not seeing someone else are you? You look the type."

"I look like the type?" Of course I look like the type. I've been snogging with my best friend's girlfriend! I am the type.

"Actually, I meant the type for an elaborate ruse. So are you seeing someone else?"

"Me?" It's completely mad that she would even think that.

For a moment I think she's teasing me, but then she gives me her on-and-off smile.

She genuinely does think that I could be seeing someone else.

I shake my head. "No."

She looks at me a moment longer, then dives in over a big wave. I follow her. The water chills my head and stings my nostrils, but feels as amazing as waking up on the first day of the summer holidays. I come up to the surface and windmill my arms. I count my strokes. I keep going for twenty before I stop and look back. Tinga's not there. I have a moment of panic, then look around. She's ahead of me. She's a faster swimmer. She's probably better at everything than me.

We body surf on a few waves and then go in.

Tinga stretches out on her towel and I lean on the breakwater that's almost too hot after the cold water.

"Tinga?"

"Mmm."

"I'll come clean about it. I know it sounds mad, but I have this fear of turning out like my old man." I pick up a shell and rub my thumb over its rippled back. "I know you think it must be cool to have him as a dad with him being a black belt and a stunt man, but that's only one side of him." I roll over to face her. She has her eyes closed and her mouth just looks so nice that I really want to kiss her, even though it would be the worst thing for me to do. "He's a total bastard, and I don't want to do any of the things he does. I feel like if I hadn't come along, you would still be with Malcolm, so from that point of view, I stole you away from Malcolm."

I toss the shell towards the water. "Stealing somebody else's girlfriend is exactly the kind of thing my old man would do, and I think that if I start behaving like him, then I'll end up like him. I mean, according to the laws of genetics, we're supposed to end up like our parents. I think you should go back to Malcolm, and just pretend that I never came along."

Tinga rolls over on her towel and props herself on her elbows to face me. "You're right."

"You mean you agree with me?"

"No. You're right about it sounding a little mad. I think you're close to being locked up for your own safety."

"Yeah. You're not the first person to point that out." I swish a finger around in some tiny rocks and pull out a piece of green sea glass. I throw it away.

"Jay. I know it's hard for you, but you aren't the only kid whose parents split up. Ask your friends. How many kids in your class have divorced parents? They say that one in three marriages end in divorce. If there are twenty kids in your class, then it's a fair bet that six of them have divorced parents."

"Six point three recurring."

"Yeah, you're probably the point three recurring. Jay, is that really what's bugging you? You don't want to be like your dad because he's a bit of a jack-the-lad, isn't he?"

"Yeah. In a nutshell."

"Nutshell is just about right."

"So, then you probably don't want to be going out with a lunatic?"

"Jay, I think I already knew you were a bit bonkers. Seriously, I don't think you're mad, just a bit of an eccentric. In fact, I half think you might be one of the most sane people I've ever met. It's part of your personality that I like about you. I like that you're a little deep and intense. I like that you think a lot about things. You're very sensitive. Most of the boys I know are idiots, but you're different. C'mon. Just let go." She looks over at the case. "Leave your dad's baggage behind."

She gets onto her hands and knees, crawls over to me on all fours, and leans on the breakwater next to me. She reaches behind me and runs her fingers through my hair as if she's washing it, but without any soap.

"Do you like this?"

It feels even better than diving into the sea. "Yeah. It's okay."

"Do you know what used to turn Malcolm on?"

"No. I'm not sure I want to know either."

"It's just this." She stops massaging the back of my head,

lifts my arm and plants little kisses on the underside of my wrist.

"That doesn't do it for me. Try the other thing again."

She does.

"Wait a minute." She freezes. "Maybe I shouldn't say this."

"No. It's okay. You might as well tell me now that you've started."

"Please don't take this the wrong way, but you're not doing this because you're afraid of Malcolm taking some kind of revenge on you or something?"

I think about the phone call, and I think about him showing me the tornado kick. "No. I'm not saying he couldn't if he wanted, but I don't think he would. Deep down I'm still a Catholic at heart, and I'm motivated only by the purest feelings of guilt."

"Really?"

"Yeah. If I thought he was going to come after me, it would change everything."

"Let me get this straight. If Malcolm is just going to stay home and mope, then you're going to go ahead and break up with me, but if he's going to come after you and beat you up, then you'll stay with me."

"That pretty much sums it up."

"Jay. You really are barmy. What if I don't want to go back to him?"

"Can't you just try?" I pick up a handful of tiny rocks and throw them one at a time at a big rock a few feet in front of me. They all miss.

"Jay. For fuck's sake. This is the absolute truth. I did not chuck Malcolm for you. I split up with him because I wanted to move on. I'm not going to go back to him. Can you get that through your thick head?"

"Okay. Okay."

"Okay, what!?"

"Then don't go back to him." I throw a whole handful of the rocks at the same time, but they still all miss. "You're right. I shouldn't try to force you to do that. If Malcolm wants to beat me up, that's just between him and me."

"Jay. Please, please, I hope that you're just pulling my leg here, and that you've actually started seeing someone else. Because if what you're telling me is even fractionally true, then you really are a basket case."

"No. I'm not seeing anyone else, and I probably am a basket case."

"So this is it then." She springs to her feet, picks up her towel, and dries her hair. "Do you have any idea what I had to go through to come out and meet you this afternoon?"

"Not really. No."

"Yesterday evening I was sitting in my room with a book on my lap, not reading it because I was so happy after seeing you. Then the doorbell rang. Somehow I knew it was trouble. We don't get a lot of callers, especially not on a Saturday night.

"Next thing I hear Malcolm's voice downstairs. Right downstairs in my house. Malcolm telling my dad that he loves me. Can you imagine? My mum and dad had no idea

I'd been seeing someone while I was walking the dog. They trusted me even though they didn't want to."

She throws the towel into the air.

"Malcolm's dad drove him to my house. I didn't even know that Malcolm knew where I lived. He knew the street, but not the house."

So that was what the shouting was about. It was about me and Tinga.

She leans forward, brushes out her hair, then flicks it back over her shoulder. "Look, Jay. I'm not going to go into the whole story, but I only got out today because I got my friend Denise to ring my house and say there was an extra choir practice at church. And it's no good ringing me tomorrow and saying you've changed your mind."

"It's okay, I won't," I say. "Listen, I know I'm doing the right thing for both of us."

She steps into her jeans, pulls on her shirt, and then puts her jacket on over it without buttoning the shirt. "I hope one day you realize how much you've hurt me. You have no idea how to treat girls, do you?" She pushes her feet into her shoes.

Only girls? I think about Malcolm, Dad, Hugh, and even *Mother!* "I don't think I have much of an idea how to treat anyone."

"I'm going back towards Wish Park. You're probably going the other way, right?"

"Right."

She takes three paces up towards the esplanade, then turns one last time. "Have a nice life."

"I'm sorry."

"Me too."

She makes her way up the beach, buttoning her shirt as she walks, then disappears into a crowd of language students in yellow rain slickers. One of the boys glances at Tinga as she passes, then looks at his friend and grins.

My dad's case looks like something that's washed up after a storm.

I really am on my own now.

SEVENTEEN

The walk to Granny Smallfield's is all uphill, but I find a number of inventive ways to carry the heavy suitcase.

I have the jungle-porter style I already practiced with Tinga.

I can carry it with both hands on the handle while it bangs against my shins.

I can lift it and carry it against my stomach, which blocks my view of where I'm going. It's a little like being on the back of the motorbike.

I could carry it on my head African-style, except that there's something inside the case with a sharp edge. This mysterious sharp object is right at the point of balance, and sticks into the top of my head.

Finally I get to her tower block above Saint Anne's Gardens, and it's only when I'm actually in the entry hall that I realize that Tinga was right. I could have just left the case on the beach and absolutely nobody would have been the wiser. Now that I'm here, I might as well see the thing through.

I drag the case through the lobby and into the elevator, then from the elevator down the hall to her door.

The bell makes an old-fashioned jingle, the same as the Briscoes, which is a little strange in the ultra-modern tower block. It's a little sad to pile old people into a modern tower block when they'd probably be much happier in old houses.

The door opens and Granny Smallfield's head appears.

"Hector?" she says, and puts a blue-veined hand up to her face.

"It's Jay, Granny." I've never seen an old person look frightened before. It's heartbreaking and unnerving at the same time.

I'm a bad grandson. I haven't seen her since my twelfth birthday. I'm only two years older now, but she looks about ten years older, which is the opposite of what you'd expect. I hold up the case. "I've brought some of Dad's things over."

"Yes, yes." She puts her hand down and smiles at me. "Come in."

I take one step into her hallway, and step back into my childhood. The furniture is all the same. The grandfather clock still makes its deep clunking tick. The little icon of Jesus with a stab wound in his chest. There are still rows of photos in black-and-white, and washed-out-yellow color photos with too-bright reds. Men, women, and children in old-fashioned clothes and uniforms. Group shots with everyone lined up according to height, and another of a family sitting in a field with an ancient black-and-chrome car in the background.

"Thank you so much for bringing those things with you."

She leads me through to the living room. I sit in the same spot on the same couch as if the years haven't passed since the last time I came here. The twenty-inch telly is a newcomer though.

"Sit down, Jay, darling," she says. "Do you want tea or coffee?"

"Tea, please." I think it's the safer bet.

"How did you cut your lip?"

"I fell off my bike."

"Bikes are awfully dangerous. I'm all in favor of the new crash helmets now. Do you wear one?"

"No." I have a momentary vision of myself looking like a fool, riding my bike in a helmet.

"Just like your father. No regard for your personal safety," says Granny Smallfield in a matter-of-fact way.

I have this dream that one day somebody is going to make a comparison between me and dad in a positive light. Wouldn't it be a treat to hear, *Oh, you are so generous, just like your father.* Or maybe, *You're so intelligent, just like your father.* Or maybe even, *You're so loyal, just like your father.*

I suppose it's a long shot.

"You have to understand that it's all very good to risk breaking your neck every day, but there are some people who actually care about you." Granny spins on her heel and heads off to the kitchen to make the tea.

According to Hugh, Granny Smallfield is the repository of all the facts about my parents' early married years, in which case the expression *just like your father* is loaded with double meanings. I'd like to ask her some questions. I try to work out exactly what the questions are while I listen to the sound of the electric kettle and the chink of cups.

A few moments later she rattles in with a tea tray, and my whole childhood comes back. I think of all those endless afternoons sitting at my grandfather's old desk, copying pictures of dinosaurs from the *Encyclopedia Britannica*.

"It's so nice to see you, Jay. You were here all the time when you were a little boy."

"I know. I used to like coming here."

Funny the things you lose when your parents separate.

"You should come and visit now and again," says Granny Smallfield. "You don't need to wait to be invited."

You don't expect to lose your only grandparent because it gets awkward.

"But Dad's living here now."

I look around, but there's no evidence that he does live here. Talk about a small footprint.

"He is still living here, isn't he?"

But she ignores me. I suppose one of the advantages of being old is you can pretend to be deaf.

"I saw your brother a few days ago. He thinks you have a girlfriend."

I almost drop the cup. He comes here? If he does come here, when does he talk about me?

I want to feel outraged, but it's hard to feel anything like that here. It's almost like Granny Smallfield's house is a place out of time. It's not part of the real world.

"I did, but we broke up."

She pushes out her lower lip as she eases herself back into her chair.

"Oh, Jay. That's very sad." She takes a sip of her tea. "I think girlfriends are probably a bit like making pancakes. The first one or two never work out very well."

"Yes." Her comparison makes me laugh, even though in my case I don't expect there are going to be any more girlfriends.

"My first boyfriend didn't work out very well either." She places her cup back on its saucer. "But you don't want to hear those old stories, do you?"

To be honest, I don't want to hear about any of her boyfriends, but then I feel that listening to her story would be *nice*, and I need to do something *nice* to make up for all of the storm trooper–like things I've been doing, so I say, "No. Tell me."

She drinks some more tea, and then says, "Well, it was in June 1943. It was a lovely day so the manager let us go home early. There wasn't much business in those days anyway. I'd just got home, and I'd just put the kettle on for tea, and Mrs. Fentiman shouted up from downstairs that there was a raid. I thought she was off her rocker because I hadn't heard a siren, so I said I was just going to finish making my tea, and she said, *It's a lightning raid, get down to the shelter, you stupid girl.* She sounded so frantic, that I just dropped everything and hurtled back downstairs to the street.

"Everybody was running, so I just joined in. I heard an old codger say, *It's a squadron of Messerschmidts. Came in under the radar. Shouldn't be allowed.* That made me laugh, but then all of a sudden there was this roar. I looked up and this plane shot right over my head. It was a huge blue thing with black crosses on the wings. The next moment I felt like I was being squeezed really tight. I couldn't breathe. There was this horrific thud. Then there was a searing hot blast of air, and then it went quite cold. Someone squeezed my shoulder and said, *Are you alright, love?* I realized I was sitting down. I was sitting right in the middle of Elm Grove and it was snowing.

"I looked around to see who'd squeezed my shoulder. It was a boy, a bit older than me, and he was covered in white stuff. It wasn't snow of course; it was cinders. *Let's get you to the shelter,* he said. He held onto my hand to help me up. I ran with him to the shelter, which was the crypt under St. Ethelburger's Church, and we stayed down there till the all-clear.

"When we came up, the air was still full of ash and it hurt to breathe, but we stopped feeling sorry for ourselves when we found out the Astoria Cinema had been hit. Forty people killed just like that. I looked down and we were still holding hands. He hadn't let go the whole time. Anyway, we spent the rest of the evening together. We walked all the way to the harbor and back, and he didn't let go of my hand once. I thought that was it. I was going to have to marry him or something, and I didn't even like him that much. But he dropped me off at my flat and I never saw him again. You probably don't want to hear these old stories though, do you?"

When she finishes, I realize I've been holding a biscuit in front of my mouth so tightly that it's snapped in half. I look out of the window, and I'm almost surprised to see it's a sunny evening. "Was that it? I mean, did you really never see him again? He could still be alive."

"No." She shakes her head slowly. "No. He was killed in the Ardennes in 1945. His name's on the war memorial down by the pier. I went and looked at it a couple of times." She shrugs. "But only because I thought I should. The week after the raid I met someone else," she laughs. "And he only lasted a few days. You think there won't be another, but take my word for it. There's going to be lots of them. You'll take after your grandfather."

My grandfather? I've never really felt like I had a grandfather.

"It's a shame you never got to meet your grandfather. He was a distinguished-looking man."

She takes another slurp of tea and there's a pause. Maybe this is the moment. If I don't ask now, it might be ages before I get another chance. But what am I going to ask?

"I was wondering."

"Yes."

"Mum and Dad's marriage. They had problems for a long time didn't they?"

"I know it's hard to believe, but they were so much in love when they were first together."

"But did they both have affairs with other people?"

"To tell you the truth, I'm not really sure what happened." She puts her cup back in the saucer. "I really think that your parents' marriage was doomed from the start. Trevor was away so much with his films, and I know that your mother got very overwhelmed being left by herself with you and Hugh when you were tiny." She takes another sip of her tea. "You know, a lot of married people have affairs, but the big difference between now and a few years ago is that, these days, an affair didn't always lead to divorce." She finishes her tea, and places the cup on the side table. "So these days an affair might be more of an excuse for divorce than a reason."

"You mean that *Mother!* and Dad would probably have got divorced sooner or later, even if Dad hadn't had an affair?"

"That about sums it up." She shuffles forward to the edge of her chair and stands up. "Just my opinion of course." She reaches a hand towards me. "Let me take your cup if you're finished."

I spring to my feet. "It's okay. I'll take the cups and wash them."

"No, dear." She takes the cup from me. "Next time. Why don't you take your father's things into the spare room?"

I lift the case for what I hope is the last time. The spare room is down the hall past the kitchen. I bang my shins on the case as I follow her, which is a slow process as Granny Smallfield is not about to break the land-speed record.

"My grandfather was Hector, right?" I ask at the kitchen doorway.

She turns and smiles at me. "Yes, that's right."

"Why did you call me Hector when I came to the door?"

"Oh. I'd just woke up from a nap when you called. I get all disoriented when I nap in the afternoon. Takes me a minute to realize where I am. But the thing about you, Jay, is that when you stand in the light in a certain way, you look exactly like him."

"My grandfather?"

"Yes. Just for one moment I thought you were him. Don't look so worried. You could do a lot worse."

A lot worse? I'm not sure what that's supposed to mean. Worse in looks? Worse in personality? Was he good at letting his friends down? I can't really question Granny's statement without offending her.

"I'll put the case in the spare room then."

I drag it through to the spare room. It looks like a monk lives there. I hadn't thought of Dad as a monk. Actually it looks more like nobody lives there.

All that's in the room is a bed, a nightstand, some shelves with a few Danielle Steel paperbacks, a picture of a vase of flowers, and another picture of some sort of forest. I half expect to see a Messerschmidt roar past the window, but there's just a view across the rooftops down to the beach.

I pick up one of the Danielle Steel books. The cover shows a girl in a bridesmaid's dress being dragged off by a man in a kilt. I try to make a mental picture of Dad reading it. Pretty difficult. In fact, it's not that easy to imagine Dad reading any kind of book. It's like trying to picture him wearing shorts, or smoking a pipe, or even living in this room.

If I'm going to find an excuse for not visiting Granny

Smallfield, I don't think I can use the old chestnut that Dad lives here in the future.

I heft the case onto the bed.

I'm halfway out the door when a fit of curiosity about Dad seizes me. I place the suitcase down flat, flip the catches open, and let out a long whistle that, seeing as I can't whistle, is more of a long hiss.

The case is full of yellow boxes of different shapes, and there's a book near the bottom. But what really catches my eye, gleaming in the late afternoon light, are some old-fashioned cameras. Two of them look pretty normal. The first one I pick up is a Yashica. It's cold metal and has a bunch of dials on the front and two windows to look through. I hold it up to my eye and look around the distorted room that now has a yellowish tinge that makes me feel like my eyes have gone weird. I put it down on the carpet next to the case, and I'm relieved that my eyes go back to normal. Next to the Yashica is a Zenith, and I don't know either of those makes. The next one is a Canon, and it's the most amazing camera I've ever seen. It has a handle like a pistol, and I use that to lift it out of the case. This one is plastic and light, and even though it looks like a gun—in fact it looks like some kind of sci-fi weapon—it really is a camera. The room even looks pretty normal through it. I lay it on the carpet next to the other two cameras.

The last camera's pretty heavy, and when I pick it up I realize it isn't a camera at all. It just has a lens. Like the gun-camera, it has a kind of old, sci-fi look. It has arms and catches, and I reckon it folds out into something. Maybe a stand. I don't know. A couple of years ago I would have played with it and broken it, but now I'm going to leave it for someone who knows how it works.

The yellow boxes all contain film. Some of them look like they're open, but I leave them shut. I have a feeling you're not supposed to expose film to light but, like the folding camera, I'm not sure how it works so I push it to one side.

At the bottom of the case is something I do understand. It's a photo album with a fake crocodile-skin cover. At least I hope it's fake.

I skim through it from the back.

I suppose there might be some conscious reason I look from the back. Like if it's Dad's album, then any pictures of me must be towards the end, but really that's not what's on my mind.

The end pages are blank; just plain black paper.

After that there are a few pages with little white triangles where somebody's removed the photos.

The first actual picture I come to is a large black-and-white one of Dad, hands on hips, in the middle of an empty room wearing karate *gi* and a black belt. He looks really pleased with himself. He doesn't look much older than Hugh, and he has his hair in a ponytail. I remember the ponytail. Embarrassing or what?

The next spread has a bunch of snaps of Dad in different places with a baby, or with a little boy and a baby. There's a space where one of the pictures has been removed.

Going farther back, there are some more black-and-whites. Pictures of Dad before he was a dad—when he was just Trevor—in some of his costumes: Dad as an Imperial storm trooper without the helmet, another in the black uniform of the Imperial Guard, and then there's a close-up of him with dark, shiny stuff coming out of his mouth and a horrible gash in his forehead exposing the bone. There's even one of him in a Nazi Uniform, which looks completely fitting on him.

There's a larger one where he's with a group of blokes with Pierce Brosnan in the middle. Pierce Brosnan has his arm around Dad's shoulder, as if they're pals and they'd spent a lot of time together. I look closer and there's something not right. Dad's grinning, but there's something a little frozen about his expression. It's like he's not really that happy to have James Bond's arm around him.

There's something not right about the whole album.

Then I get it. There are no pictures of *Mother!* She must have been through the album before she gave it to me to bring over. She must have torn out all of the pictures of herself. I can't figure it out, but it must have meant something for her to take the time to do it. Maybe she just wanted to keep the ones of her.

On the next spread, nearly all of the pictures have been torn out; there are just two pictures of Dad looking very thin with long, frizzy hair. He's wearing a dinner jacket and bow tie.

Wedding pictures. The two that *Mother!* left in only show Dad.

On the next page are two big black-and-whites. On the left is a picture of someone sliding down a rope while hanging out of one of those helicopters with two rotors. The one on the right-hand page is a close-up, and you can see that the person sliding down the rope is Dad in his dinner jacket.

He turned up to get married in a helicopter?

What a pratt!

There are some pictures of the beach. Funny, the shops and cafés don't look much different than now. One or two have disappeared, so I suppose that *Mother!* must have been there.

There are several pictures of Dad with a skinny bloke who I recognize right away. Mr. Briscoe. You can see why Dad wanted the pictures taken. He looks like one of those idiot body builders, and Mr. Briscoe's a stick. There's also a woman with one of those haircuts that looks like a German helmet. In spite of the makeup, I can tell it's Mildred Briscoe. In spite of his skinniness, Mr. Briscoe did well. Mildred was a bit of alright back then.

Next up are some pictures of Dad in the back garden of Granny Smallfield's old place in Florence Road. He's standing with a wiry old bloke and Granny Smallfield, who looks exactly the same. In fact, with those National Health glasses, she looks even older than she is now.

I suppose the old bloke must be Papa Smallfield—Hector. In the first picture, he looks a lot younger, even though Dad looks more or less the same.

They're both stripped down to the waist and wearing Monty Python hankies on their heads. Papa Smallfield flexes his arm and Dad's feeling his bicep. Papa Smallfield died when Dad was fourteen. The same age as me now.

The next set is Dad's kid pictures. Birthday party, pedal car, on a bike, dressed as a cowboy, on a bench in snow-covered mountains, in a fire truck.

I'm about to skim through the last ones—formal family pics by a baby photographer—when I stop and almost drop the album. I stare at the one of Granny and Papa Smallfield standing behind Dad in gray shorts and a bow tie.

But it isn't Dad that catches my eye. It's Papa Smallfield. He must be about thirty, but I can tell from this picture that he looks exactly like me.

I suppose I must have always had this mental image of Papa Smallfield in my head. I must have seen plenty of pictures of him as kid, but this is the first time I've looked at a picture of him and felt as though I'm looking in a mirror.

The first page has two pictures that seem to be of me. The top one shows my double in World War II khaki. A head shot. The one underneath shows him with a group of guys. I look a bit of a pratt in khaki shorts, but the tank we're standing in front of is all business. I can't help smiling to myself. Something makes my neck tingle.

Granny is right. I could do worse. I could do a lot worse. Old photos are weird. I can look right into his eyes, and it's as if he's still here somehow. I have this weird feeling that I almost want to cry.

No. It's not so much that he's here—although maybe he is—it's more that I'm there.

What was Papa Smallfield thinking right at the moment this photo was being taken? Was he afraid? If he was, he didn't show it. Not in his face anyway. Maybe in his hands.

His fists are balled up at the end of his wiry arms. He didn't need to learn karate to learn how to fight, even without the guns behind him, and those guns were real. They weren't dummy weapons for stunt men to use in films.

I would have been afraid. Just looking at him, I'm afraid for him now, even with sixty years, 5,000 miles, and whatever wall that keeps the living from the dead between us.

He must have been scared, but something must have kept him there. He must have believed in something.

The tears really want to flow.

Could I do worse?

No. That's not even the right question. The right question is: Could I be one-tenth as good as Hector?

And what about Dad? What about all the jumping off buildings? All those leaps from burning cars? All the being kicked and punched? Were they all Dad's attempts to live up to his own dad?

I close up the album like it's a long book I've just finished reading. I put everything back in the case, and then I slide it under the bed so it's out of the way.

I go back out to the living room where the television's burbling.

I tell Granny Smallfield, "The case was full of cameras and film."

"Oh. That stuff." She eases herself out of her chair and stands up. The way she moves makes me think of how stiff I was after my first karate session. "I don't really want it. Where did you leave it?"

"I put it under the bed."

"Why don't you keep it?" She shuffles back towards the kitchen. "Do you want some more tea? I forgot I have more biscuits."

"No thanks. I don't want any more tea." I actually want to leave, but I feel bad. I haven't seen her for two years, and I only spent an hour with her, and half of that was spent looking through my dad's stuff.

"I'm serious." She stops in front of the icon of Jesus and turns to face me. "I think Trevor would probably love you to have his old cameras and film." She straightens the icon. "At the very least you could probably sell them for a bit of cash. That old film equipment is worth a lot these days."

"No. I don't want to sell them. We should keep them."

"So take them home with you."

"But *Mother!* will wonder why I've brought them back again. She asked me to get rid of them."

"Put them under your own bed."

She gives me a grin that makes her look like a pixie, and just for a second I can see her as a girl.

"How old were you when you met that bloke in the raid?" I ask.

"Fifteen. I'd just left school and gone out to work."

Fifteen. A year older than Tinga is now. I wonder if Tinga will remember me when she's Granny Smallfield's age. What will she tell her grandchildren about me? Maybe I won't even be important enough for a story.

"Bye-bye, Granny," I say as I stand in the doorway.

"God bless, Jason."

I walk down the hall and turn at the top of the stairs.

The door's still open and she's still watching me. I smile and wave.

Why's she watching me? Is she wondering if she'll see me again? Sometimes life seems so bloody sad. She came so close to dying in that raid. The Astoria Cinema is still in Elm Grove. They must have rebuilt it in the same spot, and there's a church about a couple of hundred yards from it. If she'd been killed then, Dad would never have been born, and neither would I. It's hard to think about.

Now, sixty-five years later, Granny Smallfield's close to dying yet again, and there's no shelter to run to this time.

EIGHTEEN

I'm in luck for once. The house is dark when I get home so I don't have to lurk in the shadows as I carry the case up to my room. I plunk it down on the bed and survey the room. Where am I going to hide the bloody thing?

After a few minutes, I've come up with no ideas to speak of, so sit down next to the case and open it up again. Maybe I'll find inspiration inside. The first item I reach for is the pistol camera. Some of the yellow boxes of film say *Movie Film* and—I admit that I'm slow—I've worked out that it's an old-fashioned movie camera, a relic of pre-video days. I wish there was some kind of instruction book. There aren't many knobs on this particular camera, but the last thing I want to do is open some door and ruin any film that might be in it. Everything's dusty. If there is film in any of these cameras, it would have been shot years ago—maybe even decades ago. I don't want to ruin a historical document. I hold the camera up to my eye and pan around the room.

My room is pretty boring, but seeing it through the lens of this camera makes it look like part of a movie. It distorts the room in an interesting way.

I have another look through the case for a manual, and while I'm moving some of the yellow boxes around, a reel tumbles out. Okay. I know what to do with this. I've seen it in films. I undo some tape, pull down a strip of the film, and hold it up to the light. I can see the row of frames. I can see the colors. I can even see people, but it's way too small to see what's actually in the frames. I know I have a magnifying glass somewhere.

A catastrophic sneeze echoes through the house.

I jump and drop the reel.

Hugh's here. He must have been asleep or something. I start to pile the stuff back into the case almost immediately so I can hide it. Then I stop. Hugh isn't going to care that I brought the case back, and maybe he knows something about it.

"Hugh," I say in a loud voice to nobody in particular.

A grunt that sounds something like *Wha?* drifts down the hall.

"Look at this."

When I hear his footsteps, I point the camera at the door. The moment he steps in, I put on an American accent and say, "Action. Porn star, Hugh Smallfield, enters the hero's room."

"Whoa!" he says. "Where on earth did *you* get that?" He emphasizes the *you* in a way that I find slightly insulting. As if the average fourteen-year-old could have found them, but for me to acquire them is beyond belief.

"It was in the case *Mother!* had me take over to Granny Smallfield's."

"This is unbelievable, Jay! I thought all these things vanished years ago."

"Well, I was hoping you knew what they were. That's why I called you."

He stretches his arms behind his head and yawns. "Don't you remember these? No. Maybe you were too small." He holds out his hand and I give him the pistol camera. "It's Dad's old super eight film stuff. He used to take them out at Christmas. Then *Mother!* complained that everyone was bored with looking at them, so he stopped." He gives me back the camera and takes a stack of boxes out of the case, examining each one.

"I tried that," I say.

He takes a reel out of its box, unwinds some of the film, and holds it up to the light. "You've seen them though. I think the last time must have been when I was—I don't know—seven or so. Actually, it was originally Papa Small-field's stuff. You never knew about it?" He nods and rewinds the film.

I shake my head.

He sits down on the bed and starts picking through the case. "Look." He pulls out the other weird camera-type thing. "This is the projector." With swift moves, he unfolds two arms from the bodywork and places the reel he was looking at on one of the arms. "We could look at these. Was there a cable or something?"

"No. Everything that was in the case is still there."

"Are you sure?"

I roll my eyes up to the ceiling. "I'm fourteen. Not four."

"Okay, okay. Keep your shirt on. It must still be in the attic then." He yawns, places the projector on the bed, and starts looking at the film boxes again. "Dad made some films when he was your age. Actually, he and Derek Briscoe. They made a cops-and-robbers one, and a vampire one. I thought they were brilliant when I was a kid. They're probably kind of awful now, but I wish the cable was here so we could watch them."

"Maybe we could go up into the attic and have a look."

"Yeah, but not now. *Mother!*'s going to be back in a minute, and she'd have a fit. Maybe the films aren't so terrible. Dad showed them to someone to get him his first job."

"Wow. Are there some of his early stunts on these then?"

"No," says Hugh. "No stunts. He never set out to be a stunt man. He wanted to be a director. Didn't you know that?"

I shake my head.

He yawns again. "Sorry, I can't wake up. Anyway, you can't just start out as a director, so he had to start as a PA, which is a general dogsbody. He was going to have to spend years doing the jobs nobody else wanted to do until he could wangle his union card. The story he told me was that he was working on a television program about pirates and they needed somebody to jump off the mast-top of an old sailing ship into the sea—it was about twice as high as the highest board at the swimming pool. Dad volunteered, he made the jump, then had to do it twice more, and from then on he was a stunt man."

"So the story about *The Man With Golden Gun* being his first film wasn't true."

"Well, that was a couple of years later, and he just told people that because it was the first thing he was in that was famous." Hugh puts the camera back in the case, closes it, and turns to me. "So, that was your honey this afternoon?"

"Oh. Um, yeah. Well, she sort of is."

"*Sort of?* What do you mean?"

"It's a long story."

"I'm listening."

I puff out my cheeks, then mumble, "Tinga." I sit down on opposite side of the case. "The girl." How do I say this right? "She's actually Malcolm Briscoe's girlfriend."

Hugh rolls backwards off the bed and hits the floor with a thud.

"Hugh?" I stare at his big socks up on my bed, with the big toe poking out of each one. "You alright?"

Then he screams, *Aaaaaaarghhhh!*

His red face appears over the edge of the bed.

"You stole Malcolm's girl, you little bugger," he says. He slides his feet off the bed. "I don't know which fact is more amazing." He doesn't get up, just slides back so he can lean on the wall under the window. "You stealing Malcolm's squeeze," he says as he pulls his socks back up, which have slipped down, "or Malcolm having a girlfriend for you to steal in the first place."

"Wait a minute." I turn around so I can look him right in the eye. "Why are you so amazed that he had a girlfriend?"

Hugh starts to laugh, then stops himself. Probably because he sees I'm not. "Nothing. I'm just winding you up." Hugh straightens out his legs, then folds them so he's sitting in a cross-legged position.

"No. Seriously," I say.

"What exactly are you getting at?" His face is still red, but he looks different now, and I realize how rarely I see him looking serious.

"Dad told me that Malcolm tried to molest you in the shower."

Hugh sticks his hands in his armpits. "I wish I'd never said anything. I really do. I mean, I was fourteen and he was twelve. He was a little kid." Hugh spreads his arms out as if to demonstrate the short span of a twelve-year-old's life. "He probably had no idea what he was doing. I only told Dad because I thought it was funny." Hugh screws his face up and continues. "And he went ballistic. I mean, I didn't care if he was gay or not, but from what you say it seems he isn't after all."

I'm just about to tell Hugh that Malcolm tried the same thing on me, but I stop myself. Maybe it's something to do with what happened when Hugh told Dad. I don't think Hugh's going to *go spare*, but he might tell Dad, and the last thing I want is for Dad to hear that yet another son has been groped by the same boy. After all the terrible things I've done to Malcolm, it's one bit of loyalty I could show him.

Papa Smallfield would have kept it to himself. I'm pretty sure of that.

Hugh unfolds himself, stands up, and scratches his arse. "So does he know about you and—what was her name—Tinga?"

"No, I don't think he knows."

"She didn't tell him then?"

"No."

Hugh throws himself back on the bed again. "Is everything okay though? You look worried."

I shake my head.

"He was your friend, right?"

I nod.

"And if he does find out, he's going to hunt you down like a dog and kick you in the goolies with his choppy-socky?"

"No. I don't think so. He told me the karate moves he had planned for the bloke who stole Tinga, but I don't think he would really do anything."

"From the little I know about Malcolm, I'm not sure I'd completely agree with you about that." Hugh pulls a pained grimace. "But let me tell you something, Jason of the Argonauts." He leans over to me. "I had a good look at her. Even if Malcolm put you in hospital for a month, she'd be worth it."

"It doesn't make any difference now," I mumble. "I'm not going out with her anymore either."

"Hooooowat!" He bounces on the bed. "She had a fling, she chucked Malcolm, then she dumped you!? I take it back. Maybe she isn't worth it."

"I chucked *her*."

Hugh tucks his chin into his neck again. "Sunshine. Whatever planet you are from, a boy like you does not chuck a girl like her." Now I get the finger-wagging treatment. "You gratefully receive whatever she cares to bestow upon your humble personage until she moves on. Why in the name of all that's holy did you dump her? Were you afraid of Malcolm beating you up? He's going to do that anyway if he finds out. I mean, it's like robbing the bank of England. It doesn't matter if you give the money back, they'll still throw you in jail for the rest of your life whether you keep it or not, so might as well keep it."

"Hugh. I didn't chuck her because I was scared of Malcolm. I chucked her and told her to go back to Malcolm because I thought that stealing someone else's girlfriend was just the kind of devious thing that Dad would stoop to, and I want to be a better person than him."

Hugh backs away as if I've just become contagious. He opens his mouth to make some sarcy comment, but this time it's my turn.

"Look." I tap the lid of the case with my finger, as if the heart of the matter is in there—and maybe it is. "As long as I can remember, everyone has told me I'm just like Dad. Everything I do." I put on a squeaky voice. "*Oh, you're just like your father.* And it isn't intended to be complimentary. I'm sick of it. I go light years out of my way and take unbelievable measures to be different than him, and still people say, *Oh, you're just like your father.*"

"Jay," he says, "you're not well. You know that, don't you?"

"When I was over at Granny Smallfield's, she told me I was just like Dad because I don't wear a crash helmet when I ride a bicycle." I slap the top of the case. "How much more do I have to do before someone says to me, *You are nothing like your father?*"

"Well, there you go. Start wearing a crash helmet on your bike."

"Hugh. I'm being serious."

"Come to think of it, if Malcolm's after you, you might want to wear a helmet even when you're not on your bike."

I pick the case up and hold it above my head as if I'm going to throw it at him.

"Jay, calm down." He holds up his forearm across his face. "Yes. Okay. Maybe stealing someone else's girlfriend is the kind of thing that Dad might have done."

"Good. I'm glad you agree with me for a change."

"No. I'm not. Listen. What I'm trying to say is that it's the kind of thing that everyone does once in a while. All's fair in love and war—or something like that."

"So you don't think I did the right thing?"

Hugh shakes his head. "If you never stole someone else's girlfriend, then you'd probably never be able to have a girlfriend. That's how it works. If you go out with Tinga, chances are you're not going to be with her for the rest of your life. At some point someone else is going to steal her away from you." Hugh leans closer to me now. "Another girl might come along and steal you away from Tinga."

"So what's the point?"

"*What's the point?* How am I supposed to know? Who do you think I am? Socrates? Plato? Einstein? It's the way of the world. When you start going out with someone, you accept the possible consequences and so do they. If you ride a bicycle far enough, you'll eventually fall off it!"

"Well, it's done now. She says she doesn't want to see me again."

"Jay, listen to me. I will bet you any amount of money that she will not go back to Malcolm. Girls rarely go back out with blokes they've chucked. Even if he would take her back after she cheated on him. Get on the blower right now, before *Mother!* comes back, and beg Tinga on your hands and knees. No. Beg while lying prostrated on your face in the mud in the back garden. Tell her you don't know what came over you and you want to start all over again."

"You really think I should do that?"

"Yes." Hugh latches the case and puts it in his lap.

"Do you think it'll work?"

He shakes his head. "I don't know. I really don't."

"I mean, you said girls don't go back."

"Girls don't go back with blokes after they dump them, but you chucked her. There's a big difference. You are unfinished business for her. Look, I'm not giving you any guarantees, but if you don't at least try, then you'll be kicking yourself the rest of your life—that is, if there's anything left to kick after Malcolm's finished kicking you."

"I can't ring her up. I don't know her number. And before you ask, I don't know where she lives either. I mean, I know her street, but not which house she lives in. All I know is where and when she walks her dog every day."

"So go there right now. Camp out all night and wait for her. Look." He lifts up the case. "Just to make sure, I'm going to hold on to this camera equipment until you tell me you've done what I say."

"Wait. That's mine. You can't do that!"

"Oh really. I thought we shared everything, you know, like magazines. Why not cameras?"

NINETEEN

Hugh takes the case back to his room. A few minutes later he goes downstairs and switches on the telly.

As for me, I don't move from my spot on the bed for a long time.

If even half of what he's said is true, then I really have been a complete tosser.

Okay. So stealing someone else's girlfriend isn't the worst offense in the world. Even stealing a friend's girlfriend doesn't make me a storm trooper, or at least doing it once doesn't. Doing it all the time might be a different matter, and it doesn't change things between me and Dad. I'm still not going to be like him.

I have to take Hugh's word for it, because the only other people I know who know anything about this kind of thing are Tinga and Malcolm, and obviously I can't ask them. Hugh's capable of being a bit of a bastard when he wants to be, but deep down I don't think he would pratt around when something this serious is in the cards.

The hardest part of the whole thing is not so much admitting that Hugh is right, but actually telling him to his face that he's right. In the event Hugh takes it pretty well. No crowing. No *I told you so*. To top it all, when I tell him about my bike, he even puts his money where his mouth is and offers me a lift over to Wish Park.

This is something of an eye-opener. Hugh takes a completely different route than the one I've been taking, and I'm barely settled in on the pillion before we get there. Turns out, it's barely three miles. Up till then, I'd been following the bus route which—as Hugh says—goes all around the houses and is about twice the distance.

The knowledge that I haven't been so far away from Wish Park all along gives me this feeling, deep down, that it's all going to work out. I give Hugh a farewell slap on his crash helmet and breeze into the park from the seafront end.

The playground is empty, apart from a crazy bloke who's muttering at the park keeper's little hut, and one of the skinheads.

I should probably worry a little about the skinhead, but he isn't Narrow-face. He's on his own and so there's nobody for him to impress. I glance over at him, and he's giving me the evil eye, but he doesn't get up or anything.

Then I see Tinga over by the tennis courts. I sprint until I'm about twenty yards behind her, then I slow to a walk. I don't want be all out of breath when I reach her. She's wearing clothes I haven't seen before and I don't know where Rosko is. I walk quickly until I'm ahead of her, then notice she's not wearing glasses. It's not her. It's a woman of about thirty.

"Can I help you?" she asks.

"Sorry, I thought you were somebody else," I say.

There's a shelter on a little rise just to the north of the bowling greens, and I go and sit in there.

And I sit.

I don't know if the tennis court clock's right, but it passes four.

I suppose it could be fast. Or maybe Tinga's been delayed by something.

I sit and wait until four fifteen, which seems like an age.

Then I see her. This time I wait. She has a dog, but this one is a Dalmatian. I watch until I can see her face. She's not the least bit like Tinga. What was I thinking?

It starts to rain, so I go and hang out in the shelter. It's on a slope behind the playground, and it gives me a full view of the park. I see a few more dog walkers, but not the one I'm looking for. Then I see the one dog walker I'm not looking for. Malcolm.

I could go over to him and set things straight, but something more than the rain keeps me in the shelter. Seeing him wandering about on the empty football field in the drizzle makes me feel awful. I really am going to take his girlfriend away from him now, and I have no idea what I could say to him to make things better.

My upbeat feeling drains out of me.

I slide into the shadows of the shelter. By the time Malcolm's gone, it's probably close to five, and it's time for me to make the long walk home.

The next day is Monday, so I have to wait till after school to go to the park. I don't want to get into a discussion about it with anyone, not even Hugh, so I walk. Walking actually takes less time than I expect, but it still takes close to an hour. This time I only see one person I think is Tinga, although I see another girl who looks like her on the way home.

Once again, when I finally see them from the front, I can't understand what I was thinking.

I get back at about seven-thirty. I've been gone for about three hours. I want to go back just one more time. Third time's a charm, but I can't disappear for another three hours. I'm already way behind with my homework.

As soon as I get in from school on Wednesday, I dig out my gym plimsolls and my track-suit bottoms. I can't bike, and it takes too long to walk, but I can jog there. I leave home at half past four.

I'm gasping for breath almost before I reach Elm Grove—the half-way point. I stop and lean on a tree in front of Saint Peter's Church. A gangly middle-aged bloke jogs past me from the opposite direction. I may be imagining it, but I think he sneers at me. It's as if he's saying, *Look at me, I'm forty years older than you and twice as fit.*

Even with all the stops, I still get to the park at about ten to four. I sit in the shelter and realize that if Tinga does show up, I'm probably going to look like a bit of a pratt in a sweaty T-shirt and track-suit bottoms, but I suppose even at this stage I'm sort of ignoring the obvious truth.

I stagger back home, inhale my dinner, and fall asleep in front of the telly.

I try again the next day. I pass gangly-man at pretty much the same place, and this time I surprise myself by getting all the way to the park without having to stop, but my feet are in agony. If Tinga shows up, she'll find me sitting in the shelter with my plimsolls off rubbing my feet through my socks which, by complete coincidence, don't match.

But she doesn't show up.

On day five, I manage to run all the way to the park without much trouble, apart from the feet. In fact I pass gangly-man just before I stop to stretch. Either he's leaving home later, or I'm getting faster.

I even have enough puff left to give him a hearty, "Afternoon." He runs past me. I think he's going to ignore me, but he stops and turns around. Is he going to cave in and acknowledge me? Am I now a real runner?

"You damn fool," he says. A Yank, natch. "You'll end up in a wheelchair if you keep running in those shoes." Then he turns and goes on his way. I think about chasing him and kicking him in the arse, except that being a Yank, he'd probably shoot me.

It stands to reason, right? If my legs ache less after each run, then my feet will hurt less, but the opposite actually happens. By the time I get home on the fifth day, the soles of my feet, my ankles, and my calves are killing me. It should be gangly-man that has these old-man aches and pains. Not me.

Another lapse in apparent logic is that *Mother!* coughs up thirty quid for a pair of Nike running shoes. She even drives me to Broomfields to get them.

The next day I feel like I have an electric motor in my legs.

I don't even bother to stop when I reach Saint Peter's Church. I turn right, head west, and keep going. Instead of listening to the slap of my plimsolls on the pavement, I listen to my breathing, the traffic, and the gulls. The trainers make hardly any sound at all.

So as soon as I solve one problem, another one rears its ugly head.

My feet no longer hurt, and in fact I feel pretty good in my body, but the new problem that I have to face up to is that it's probably not mere chance that I haven't seen Tinga in her regular dog-walking spot.

She's changed her routine, and there can only be one reason she's changed her routine, now of all times.

Nevertheless, I keep running over to Wish Park, but only because I like the run. I don't go with any hope of meeting Tinga. Besides, running gives me plenty of time to think, so I make a mental list of my options. I could go to her house, but there are (and I took a running detour to check this) a hundred houses on Adelaide Terrace. So I could spend a month knocking on every door if it wouldn't have been the most sad and pathetic thing imaginable.

A marginally better option is that there are two other parks nearby, the Goldstone Grounds and the Rec. It's quite possible that Tinga has switched and walks Rosko at one of those at four o'clock. So I try them and draw a blank.

I have one option left, which is probably the worst option imaginable.

Unless her family has moved to another town because of me, which seems melodramatic even by my standards, Tinga will, come hell or high water, go to All-Fitness Karate at some point.

One evening after running, I look them up in the Yellow Pages and give them a ring.

No. They won't give out information about any individual students.

Yes, they do have teen classes every weekday at five.

Yes, anyone between the ages of eleven and eighteen can come along for a free trial class.

There are a couple of snags to this plan.

The first one is merely practical. According to Hugh, All-Fitness Karate is about a mile farther away from home than Wish Park. This works out as an eight-mile return trip. Not a marathon, but not an easy run either, especially if I'm going to stop and do a full karate workout halfway through. The other problem is this: I've studied karate, but I've never yet been in a karate class. I've watched plenty of my dad's classes from across the street, and he tends to be pretty strict. I don't think any *sensei* is going to allow me to just sit around and chat with Tinga.

Maybe I could just be a spectator and sit the class out. I think that would give me more of a chance to talk, and it would have the added advantage of giving me a bit of recuperation before my run back.

The only thing I do differently is take a jacket so I don't get chilled when I stop running.

I don't have a special running jacket, so I take my winter one. Even though it's almost June, the evenings are still cold and I'm going to freeze my arse off when I run back. The jacket's too hot to wear on the way over, so I have to tie the sleeves around my waist, which makes it look like I'm wearing a skirt. The things you do for love.

TWENTY

All-Fitness Karate is sandwiched between a junk shop and an electrician on the last block of Portland Road. It's already getting chilly so I'm glad I brought my jacket; I put it on. I hang out in a newsagent on the other side of the street and watch a bunch of kids trickle in, but I don't see Tinga. The kids are all wearing normal jackets and sweatshirts, but underneath they all have the tell-tale baggy white pajama bottoms.

Then a blue Volvo pulls up and Tinga steps out.

Over the last few days, I've seen so many false Tingas that I should be a bit cautious about thinking it's really her. But it's not my eyes that tell me this is the real Tinga. It's a sort of empty feeling with a hollow hammering in my chest. I'm not scared, but it feels a lot like being scared.

I'm not going to have a lot of opportunity to speak to Tinga, so I'm going to have to pick my moment very carefully.

I suppose if I was really ballsy, I'd run straight over to her while she's leaning back in through the car window. I wouldn't care that the stocky bloke wearing a cap and sitting behind the wheel of the car is probably her dad. I wouldn't care that he would probably jump out of the car and pummel me into the asphalt. I do care that he would probably drag Tinga back into the car and drive off, obliterating whatever chance I have left. So I bide my time, let her go inside, and let him drive away.

It also gives me a chance for a few long, slow breaths.

The moment Tinga's dad is around the corner, I jog across the street, fumble with the door handle, and go in, but I get inside just in time to see her vanish into the girls' room.

A hand grips my shoulder.

I turn around and look into the face of a bloke of about Hugh's age. Well, I don't exactly look into his face, I look into his chest, then look up into his face. I try not to stare at his nose that has a big dent in it, but the mouth underneath cracks into a smile.

"You want to do a trial class?" he asks.

I try to tell him that I'm just going to watch, but the fearlike feeling has made my mouth go dry and nothing comes out.

At the same time I glance past him to a row of folding chairs just inside the front window. All of them are occupied apart from one. The fearlike feeling gets a little more like real fear, because sitting next to the empty seat is the bloke who was staring at me that day at the beach while I was snogging with Tinga. I recognize him now. I saw him just a few days ago. At least I saw a younger version of him in Dad's photo album. He's Derek Briscoe. Malcolm's dad. He recognizes me as well, because as soon as he sees me he stands up. Ideas of frying pans and fires flip through my head.

"Yes," I tell the big bloke who, at this moment, seems to be the only solid object between me and certain death. "I'm here for a trial class."

"Brilliant," he says. His smile spreads into a grin. He has big teeth like a horse.

I don't know why he needs karate. He could just defend himself by biting people.

"Take your shoes off and put your jacket in the changing room. Then you can come out and limber up a bit." He points to three doors at the back of the dojo.

"Thanks." I make my way between stretching ninjas, touching their toes and doing the splits. No Tinga. She must still be in the girls' room.

The walk across the dojo helps me get my breath back, so I half slide my arms out of the sleeves of my jacket and push through the door marked *Boys* with my shoulder. Then the fearlike feeling comes racing back, this time with a vengeance. An all-too-familiar back is facing me. If my hands weren't trapped in the sleeves of my jacket, I'd slap myself on the forehead and say *Duh*. What was I thinking? If his dad is here, then it stands to reason that he must be too. Malcolm is right in front of me with his foot up on the wash basin, trimming his toenails. I stop halfway through the door and begin to back out, but there's a mirror on the wall above the basin. I catch his eye for half a second and he spins around.

"Jay! Where have you been hiding?" He takes his foot down from the sink. "You going to do a class?"

This is it. This is what it all comes down to. I came here to try and make up with Tinga, but right in front of me is the wall I have to get over before I can do that. Why don't I think these things through? Why wouldn't he be here? I can't say anything to Tinga without Malcolm finding out that I was the "bastard." On the other hand, I could just take the class, ignore Tinga, and walk away.

Am I a man or a mouse? Mouse definitely, but a mouse with balls. "It was me," I say, in a mouselike voice.

"What do you mean it was you?"

I swallow. "Me and Tinga," I croak.

His smile vanishes. "Are you taking the piss?"

"No." I want to slide back out through the door, but I stay there. No point in running now. "I wouldn't joke about it."

He doesn't say anything for what seems like ages, although it's probably just a few seconds.

The fearlike feeling I've been experiencing becomes almost indistinguishable from the genuine article.

There's one other boy in the room who looks about ten or eleven. He tugs his yellow belt tight around his middle, then pulls the cuffs of his *gi* so they make a snapping noise. I want him to stay, but he pushes past me and out into the dojo.

"My dad was right."

"Your dad thought it was me? How did he know?" As

the words come out, I know. Obviously. It was him I saw when I was snogging with Tinga at the bandstand.

"He said you were just a chip off the old block. He said you were just a pathetic little wanker like your old man."

"I'm what!?" A dull ache runs up my neck and into the sides of my head. "I'm what!?" Everything blurs into a kind of reddish glow. "I'm what!?" Right in the middle of that glow is Malcolm's stupid, ugly, moronic face. I shuffle my shoulders like mad, but the bloody jacket is still stuck on my arms.

"Are you completely mad? You've got a lot of nerve coming here and telling me that, Jay," says Malcolm. "I'll give you that much."

I know he doesn't mean it in a flattering way, but it's true nonetheless. I have got a lot of nerve. It sounds weird but, for one millisecond, I step out of my body, float to the other side of the room, and have a good look back at myself. For that fleeting moment I'm not a pudgy fourteen-year-old. I'm not the son of a dodgy karate instructor. I'm a scrawny bloke in an old photo from an old war. A little bloke in khaki shorts and a tin helmet with his fists balled up, waiting to punch the entire Afrika Korps on the nose if he has to.

Now I know exactly what my grandfather was thinking in the photo.

Sod 'em. Sod every last one of the arseholes!

"Too bloody right I've got nerve!"

I half expect Malcolm to scream *kee-yah* and pummel me into the yellow linoleum floor. This is not good. I might have nerve, but I still have my hands trapped in the sleeves of my jacket.

I draw a long breath in through my nose. My grandfather would have stood his ground, but he'd give the other bloke a way out, plus an apology if one was due. "Look. I'm sorry about what happened." I shrug with my arms still stuck in the sleeves of my jacket. "I want to put things straight between us."

"What a coincidence," he says, "because that's exactly what I want to do, and I have some really special moves all planned out for you." He comes over, stands behind me, and pushes the door shut, as if I was about to leave, which I wasn't. "See this poster?" On the back of the door is a Chinese-style poster showing a front and back view of a naked man. Around the edge are some Chinese symbols with arrows pointing to various parts of the man's body. "These are all the most sensitive spots where you don't have to hit hard to do a lot of damage." He taps the symbol that points to the spot just under the sternum. "Just imagine what would happen if the blow was hard."

"Lovely," I say. The nerve I had a few moments ago is beginning to fray. "I'll be aiming for the same spot on you."

"In your dreams," he says. He pulls his red belt out to the full width of his arms so it makes a snapping sound, then he wraps it around his waist. "Which hospital do you want to wake up in?"

"Same one as you," I say as I pull the door open. "Then we can just keep going."

But he steps back. The silly grin falters, fades, and then droops.

Eureka! My right hand pulls free of the sleeve.

Let's get it over with now.

But at that exact moment something solid smacks me in the back.

The door.

It could only happen to me. Only I could start a fight while I'm standing in front of a door, and this door shoves me right into Malcolm. Malcolm stumbles back and holds onto me to keep his balance.

"Girls, girls, girls!" I sweep around and, once again, look straight into the chest of the big bloke I saw when I first came in—the one with the dented nose and horse's teeth.

"Well, I never," he says. He looks from me to Malcolm, then back to me. "Romance rears its ugly head in the dojo."

TWENTY-ONE

The big bloke, whose name—it turns out—is Tyler, kicks me out of the changing room, but stays in there with Malcolm.

There's now about twenty kids stretching, although it looks like more because one wall is nothing more than a huge mirror. I notice a couple of the girls are in full splits. It actually hurts to watch.

I glance over to the seats by the window. Mr. Briscoe scowls at me, and the seat next to him is still empty.

My narrow window of opportunity to speak to Tinga has just got narrower. Now I'm probably going to have to do it with Malcolm breathing down my neck.

Every one of the students is wearing an immaculate white *gi* except for me, of course, in my blue T-shirt and sweat pants. Nobody's talking and the only sound is heavy breathing.

I'm the oddball, as usual.

The spirit of my grandfather, or whatever it was that took control of me back in the changing room, is now gone. It's as if he was never there in the first place.

I no longer have nerve. I just feel self-conscious standing around, so I copy the bloke nearest to me, a yellow belt. He bends forward with a red face. His spreads his feet wide apart, then twists to one side and holds onto his ankle. This gives me a chance to look around from a knee-high perspective.

There's one more dad. This one stands on the opposite side to where the other parents are sitting. He has his arms folded across his thick chest, and his face is crumpled into the sweetest smile I think I've ever seen on a grown-up. At first I wonder why he isn't sitting with the other parents. Then I figure out who he is and it makes sense. I follow his gaze and I see his daughter, practicing kicks in the mirror. The reason I didn't recognize her is that she's wearing different glasses, the thick black-rimmed, government-issue style with a strap that goes around the back of her head. Her hair is pulled into a ponytail that bounces up and down when she kicks. I can't take my eyes off the view of her from behind.

I look back at her dad. If only he knew how much we had in common. Well, probably only one thing actually.

I look back at Tinga. Everything—the glasses, the back view, the bouncing ponytail—focuses my gaze on her ears.

Then she stops. I look at the reflection of her face in the mirror and she's staring right at me. She looks like she's watching a multiple car crash—and maybe she is. It must be her way of repeating exactly what Malcolm said, *What the heck are* you *doing here?*

Maybe I'm wasting my time. Maybe I should just get my things and bolt. This is really stupid. I can't fight Malcolm, and what am I even going to say to Tinga.

On the other hand, I've come all this way. I have to at least try, and this is very much it. My opportunity. I'm not going to be able to speak to her during class, and I don't know what shape I'm going to be in at the end of the class. It's a one-shot, and there are three people in this room who probably want to kill me. Malcolm, of course; his dad, probably; and her dad. The one ace I have up my sleeve is that her dad doesn't know who I am, but he probably will as soon as I start speaking to her.

It's suicidal insanity, so I take a deep breath, stand up, and walk over to her.

"Tinga," I say.

She stops kicking and clasps her hands to the top of her head as if it's going to fly off. With her sweaty red face, the geeky glasses, and the ponytail, she looks even lovelier than the image I've been pasting onto just about every female I've laid eyes on over the last couple of weeks.

"I have to speak to you." I don't know how long I have for my little speech, so I babble the whole thing out. This isn't helped by the fact that I'm as out of puff as if I've just done a hundred push-ups, even though all I've done is stretch. "I've really missed you, *puff*. I'm sorry, *puff*. I did the wrong thing, *puff*. I know you said I shouldn't try to see you, *puff*, but I want to get back together with you."

I have no idea how she'll respond. She might even give

me one of the kicks she's been practicing. But her face just gets redder.

"I've missed you too, Jay," she says in a loud whisper, "but we can't talk now." She takes the band off her ponytail, then pulls her hair back tighter and refastens it.

"Well, when?"

"Please go away." She glances over my shoulder.

I turn around to see her dad making his way around the two or three students who are in between us.

A door bangs behind me.

Everyone freezes like it's a game of statues at a children's party. Including Tinga's dad.

"Class!" A female yell explodes right behind me. Loud enough to make my ears ring. "Grab your ropes and line up!" The voice carries such force that I don't even dare to look around.

Twenty statues—me included—spring into action, running in different directions, but mostly towards a rack of jump ropes.

Tinga grabs my shoulder. "The park tomorrow."

"Okay."

She gives me a smile. It's not even much of a smile, but I'd let Malcolm jump up and down on my face all night for that smile. I give her a quick smile back, but that's all I have time for.

A West Indian woman with her hair in braids marches past me. She goes up to the windows. Tyler bows to her and shouts, "*Hooss!*" She bows to him then comes back and stands in front of the middle door. Her *gi* are black. Her black belt has so many gold bands on it, they almost go all the way around her waist. Her jacket is festooned with embroidered badges showing little symbols of fists, Japanese characters, and silhouettes of people kicking other people in the face.

Without my noticing, the class has arranged itself into four rows. Except for me—of course. I shuffle over and stand in front of a boy with a red belt.

"Good afternoon, class!" The *sensei* leaves about a second's gap between each word, and even though you could hear a pin drop in the gaps, she doesn't use an indoor voice.

"Good afternoon, *Sensei*," responds the class.

Sensei places her hands in front of her crotch and yells, "*Hooss!*"

"Excuse me," says *Sensei* in the kind of voice you might use if you want the Queen to pass the ketchup at a garden party. She comes over and stands about a foot in front of me. She's no taller than me, and probably no heavier. Her *gi* top is open quite wide. If I let my gaze drift down from her jet-black eyes, I could probably see her bra. Not that I would ever think of doing such a thing in a million years.

"Yes," I squeak.

"Yes, *Sensei!* Are you a black belt?" she inquires as if I'm standing a couple of miles away on a wind-swept moor.

"No."

"No … *Sensei!*"

"Get to the back of the class then."

Okay. I get it. "Yes, *Sensei!*"

I glance over at both Tinga and Malcolm's dads on my way back to the window. Both give me narrow looks. Nothing in the world would stop either one of them from dragging me by my ear out onto the sidewalk and tearing me to pieces. Nothing, that is, except for the prospect of being yelled at by the *sensei*.

In spite of my being protected by the most unlikely of guardian angels, I find a spot as far away from either of them as I can get.

"Class!"

I jump.

"We'll start with a short warm-up, then stretch, and then go straight to sparring. We're going to do full-contact, so the lower belts will just watch. After that, we're going to break boards and then do forms. Let's begin with jump rope. Three minutes. Good luck to you six."

The *sensei* says all of this in about as much time as it takes to sneeze, and the moment she stops, the room is filled with the sound of jumping feet, heavy breathing, and ropes whining as they cut through the air.

The running has done more than just transport me to Wish Park. Three minutes is almost not long enough for me to warm up.

"Down for twenty," yells the *sensei*. "And count!"

"*Ichi…ni…san…shi…go…roku…shichi…*"

At *hachi* I notice a pair of brown feet in front of my face. "Take a breather, you."

I swing my feet forward so my toes line up with my fingertips then stand.

"Thank you, *Sensei*," she says.

"Thank you, *puff, Sensei*."

"You're in good shape. Have you trained before?"

I shrug. "A bit, *Sensei*."

"A *bit*! I'll give you a bit. What's your name?"

"Jason, *Sensei*."

"Do you have a belt?"

"Um … green, *Sensei*. But it was a long time ago."

"Step into your stance."

I swing my arms back and forward. "*Kee-yah!*" At the same moment, she brings her hands up to her shoulders. On each hand is a circular punching mitt.

"Punch right-to-right, left-to-left until I tell you to stop."

I throw my fists at the opposite pads. She bats my fists back with the pads as if my knuckles are Ping-Pong balls. It hurts. I miss a couple of times.

"That's enough. Thank you, green-belt Jason."

By the time I'm finished punching, the class is jumping rope again, so I pick up my rope and spin it. The *sensei* heads off to intimidate another student.

We do a fourth round of jump rope, then Tyler yells, "Stretch it out!" There's a drum roll as nineteen jump ropes are thrown to the ground, then an extra thud as the twentieth one is dropped. Mine of course.

My heart's pounding, but I'm glad to hear a lot of puffing and blowing.

Even the fittest ones are out of breath.

Tyler spreads his feet apart and bends one knee.

I slide one foot back, bend my knee like the boy next to me, and the counting begins again.

We switch legs and the boy gives me a wide grin. "That's the worst of it," he says, while everyone counts again.

Malcolm is two rows in front of me. He twists and glares at me.

All I need to do is keep well away from him.

"What do you mean?" I ask my row-mate.

"The sparring is usually pretty light," he says as he straightens one knee, twists, and bends the other. "Unless it's a test. There's usually a bit of blood. It keeps it real, but you have to be a green belt or above to spar on a test."

"*Hooss!*" *Sensei* has emerged. "*Hooss!*" shouts the class. The atmosphere changes. Everyone runs back to their place in line. "Get padded up."

"Uh oh," says the boy next to me with a wry grin. "What hospital do you want to wake up in?"

About half of the students crowd into their respective changing rooms, the rest kneel along the mirrored wall.

One student looks like a pratt standing in the middle of the floor. Well, two, if you count the real me along with my reflection. The line of kneeling—non-sparring—students has almost reached the spot where Tinga's dad is leaning in the corner. If I join that line I will be kneeling right in front of his hard-looking black shoes.

The upper belts are drifting back in, sitting on the floor, getting padded up. *Sensei* and Tyler have their arms full of sparring gear, presumably extras for those who need them.

I make a snap decision. I can't run away from Malcolm.

Now that he knows it was me who stole Tinga, he's going to get even at some point, so it might as well be now. Otherwise I'm going to have to spend the rest of my life looking over my shoulder.

"*Sensei.*" My voice shakes. I can't summon up the spirit of my grandfather to make me brave, so I'm just going to have to be brave on my own account. Maybe I can pretend to be brave. Maybe that's all being brave is. Pretending.

She turns and marches over to me.

Everything hinges on one moment. I have to do this. Quickly, before I can change my mind I ask, "Can I spar?"

She looks me up and down in just the way Malcolm did when I went to his house. When her gaze comes back to my face, she draws in a long breath, and shakes her head.

"I am a green belt, *Sensei.*"

She stops shaking her head and gives me a big grin. Then with a lightning-fast move, she pulls the head gear over my hair and fastens it tight under my chin. "Lucky you. I had to wait six months before I was allowed to punch anyone."

She squats down at my feet and fastens on the floppy, padded galoshes. "Just take it easy," she says. "It's your first time, and you're going to be nervous, but don't try to kill anyone." She laughs and fastens the mitts over my hands. "Unless you're with Tyler. You can do what you like to him." Then she adds, "You didn't bring a mouthpiece, did you?"

I shake my head.

Sensei flicks the head gear with her index finger. It makes a pop. "You'll be fine. Just keep your mouth shut, breathe through your nose, and don't bite your tongue off."

"Yes, *Sensei.*"

"Okay. Two lines!"

We form into two parallel lines that run the length of the dojo. I reckon the two lines are like two teams. Both Tinga and Malcolm are in the same line. I figure if I'm in the same line then I won't end up fighting with either of them.

But of course Tyler says, "Too many in this line." He puts a hand on my shoulder and says, "Go over to the other line."

Now my heart begins to really crank up the pace.

Malcolm is at the doorway end of his line. I make sure I'm at the window end, so there's no chance we'll meet.

"Two minutes," shouts Tyler. "Nice and light. If you hurt anyone, you fight me."

"And if you can hurt Tyler," shouts *Sensei,* "I'll buy you ice cream."

"Okay. *Go,*" yells Tyler.

The air is instantly filled with huffing and puffing, slapping noises, and cries of *kee-yah.*

I look over at my opponent. I go from feeling scared to feeling silly. She's a blue belt of about eleven. I smile at the big brown eyes I see through the slot in her head gear.

I have no idea what I'm doing. I glance to my left. A girl throws a straight left at her opponent. Her fist hits the head gear with a loud—not at all light-sounding—*Pop!*

I crouch into a boxing stance and bounce towards my opponent. I'm just about to tap her on the forehead when something hard hits me in the stomach and I end up sitting on the floor. I look up just in time to see her pull her foot back.

The kick doesn't really hurt. Maybe I can just keep doing this till the class ends. I have to admit that it is a little humiliating to be kicked onto my arse by an eleven-year-old girl, but at least I'll survive.

I haul myself to my feet and bounce forward again, and of course the same thing happens.

Pop … pop … slap … pop … slap! The girls next to me seem to be trying to kill each other in spite of what *Sensei* said. Maybe it's one of those things that has to be said, but in the actual event nobody takes any notice.

Then I see with shock that both girls are green belts, and that one has glasses inside her head gear. Tinga. As I haul myself to my feet, Tyler shouts, "Break," then my line moves down one. For one second I think this is going to bring me face-to-face with Tinga, but it's worse. I'm face to face with Malcolm.

I'm just wondering if I can keep shuffling to the left, perhaps all the way out of the door, when Tyler yells, "Go!"

"It's lights-out time," mumbles Malcolm through his mouthpiece. "Say your prayers."

But I don't have time to think of one before his foot whacks the side of my head with a loud *pop*. My eyes flash as if someone's just taken a photo. The room jumps around and I have to sit down. This time I feel like staying there, but Malcolm swings another kick at my head. I shift to the side and the kick hits me on the shoulder with a *slap*. It feels like I've stood up and banged my shoulder on a closet door I hadn't seen.

I'm not going to survive two minutes of this. I'm probably not going to survive another ten seconds.

"Pick on someone your own size, you big bra strap!"

Who said that? Am I going to be rescued?

For one second I think it's over. Someone in charge saw Malcolm kick me while I was down, and he's going to be sent off—or out—or something. But he just moved too far to the side and got mixed up with the two boys fighting next to us.

I glance around the room for help from *Sensei* or Tyler, but they're fighting each other.

Sensei has Tyler off the ground in the corner by the window and she looks as if she's using him as a punch bag.

No help from them, and no point in staying on the floor. I try to bounce to my feet, but before I'm up, Malcolm knocks me down again with a front kick that lands right where my hip joins my leg. It feels like being hit by a car.

The kick knocks me right off my feet, but it's so hard that I do a backwards somersault and land upright again. My shoulder blades are pressed against something cold and hard. The mirror.

I'm out of space, and out of time.

Malcolm moves off to one side, but before I can turn to face him, he hits me with a flurry of punches and kicks, *pop-pop-slap-pop-slap-pop*. I feel like I'm being thrown down the stairs.

I curl forward and cover my face with my mitts, but the blows keep coming. Then they stop for a second. I peep through the tiny gap between my gloves just in time to see a big and well-trimmed toenail sweep past my face. In my mind's eye, I see an image of his punch bag bending in half. This is it. The tornado kick. The finisher. All I can do is shove my left hand out to keep him off, and he headbutts my hand!

The shock goes right up my arm, and I feel my shoulder pop out of its socket.

Malcolm pulls a silly face, like it's all a big joke, then he pretends I've knocked him out. It's such a good act that he even bounces when he hits the floor.

It's such a good act that *Sensei* and Tyler stop fighting and run over.

"Stop!" bellows *Sensei*.

The entire class goes down on one knee.

Apart from me of course.

"Sorry," I say to nobody in particular as *Sensei* rolls Malcolm onto his side and Tyler pulls his head gear off.

"I've just remembered I have a dentist's appointment," I say, but nobody looks at me. I stand up, grab my shoes, and run out through the dojo into Portland Road in my bare feet.

TWENTY-TWO

I go four or five blocks before I stop and put my shoes on.

It could be worse.

It could be raining.

Even though it isn't raining, my sweat-soaked clothes cling to me in a horrible, slimy way as I start to cool down.

The sun is just over the pier. It'll be dark in ten minutes, so the sun's not going to help dry my wet stuff.

I stumble into a slow run. I watch the long shadows of my feet as they slap the pavement.

So much for specialized running shoes. At every step a different part of my body screams. My thighs hurt, my back feels like a hammer's hitting it, my stomach feels like Malcolm's foot is in it, my ribs feel like somebody's working them with a hacksaw. I can't swing my left arm and my face is expanding at about the same rate as the universe.

The worst thing of all is my neck. My head feels like it

weighs about as much as a cannon ball, and even the slight-est movement makes my neck feel like it's about to snap.

Dad once played a zombie in the movies. I can go one step further. I'm playing one for real.

I'm just thinking that perhaps I feel worse than I look, when I pass a bloke and his girlfriend leaning on a car. The girl glances at me and her face cracks into a wail I can't hear. The bloke spins around and goes into a sort of caveman stance as if he's about to beat the crap out of me if he can only find something to break that isn't already broken.

"You alright, mate?" he says.

"Brilliant," I say, only it comes out as *Fa-fa-ant* as my upper lip is now the size of a banana.

My nose is blocked so I blow it into the short sleeve of my T-shirt. It feels like my snot is made of napalm. Then I have to spit just as I pass an old guy with a yellow lab.

"Christ," he says, as I half-run half-stumble past him.

Maybe if he ran a bit he'd have a trimmer, happier pooch.

I reach Wish Park just as the sun goes down. I know it's not safe, but I need to be somewhere out of view. Somewhere I can sit for a minute and think about what to do next.

I take a sharp turn through the gates and my feet crunch on the gravel path.

There's a couple of figures on the playground ahead of me. The playground's big and I sprint through the opposite side to the figures.

My feet swish through the wet grass. I want to sit down, but I keep going. I know where I have to get to.

Just before the tennis courts is a drinking fountain. I turn the handle and the spray shoots up. I suck up a mouthful of the icy water, swish it around, then spit it out onto the ground.

I repeat this a few times, then make a cup with my hands, fill them with water, and try to wash my face. I don't know if I'm cleaning anything up, but the water's cold enough to numb me a little. My neck still feels horrible.

When I'm done, I stumble past the tennis courts and up to the shelter.

A little orange firefly dances around in the darkness.

Shit, somebody's there having a smoke. With my luck, it's probably Narrow-face, and he'll be able to finish me off.

Too bad. I have to sit down. "Sorry. Don't mind me," I say, which comes out almost like it's supposed to—the water must have done some good. I throw myself onto the bench as far away from the glow of the cigarette as I can.

I shift a couple of times to see if there's a way I can sit that doesn't hurt, realize there isn't, so I give up and look at the stars between the dark silhouettes of the trees. In fact they aren't even stars, they're street lamps on Brunswick Hill behind the park.

"Jay?"

What? A girl's voice. For a second I think it might be Narrow-face impersonating a girl, then my heart pounds.

"Tinga!"

"No, it's Siggur," comes the voice. The little orange glow dances to my left.

"Hey, Siggur." I look towards where the voice comes

from and grin, which opens up a cut in my lip so I give up. Besides, it's dark anyway so there's not much point in grinning. "How's things?"

"Kind of shitty," she says. "How about you?"

"Kind of shitty, too," I say, "but I think I prefer your kind of shitty to mine." I shift again to face where I guess she is. "Tell me about your kind of shitty."

"Ach. Man trouble. Really, you don't want to know. How about you?"

As I get used to the darkness, I can just about make her out opposite me, leaning forward with her elbows on her knees.

She blows out a lungful of smoke and says, "You look like you've been working out a lot." She coughs and taps the ash off her smoke. "You're starting to look thin and strong. You should try to stay this way."

I'm not really sure what to say to this. I can't remember a moment in my life when anybody has said anything good about how I look.

She coughs. A car passes and its headlights throw a yellow beam across her for a second. "You're not used to being complimented, are you?"

"No." I laugh. "Usually I only hear the bad things, and I'm told I'm just like my father."

"You mean your father who doesn't live at home?" She finishes her cigarette and I watch the little orange spark as it spirals out of the shelter.

"Yeah. I don't have a step-father."

"It must be difficult for you without a dad. I had the same." She cups her chin in her hands.

"No. I can't stand him. I haven't seen him for nearly two years. I'm glad he's gone."

"Jay. That's terrible." She reaches into her bag and there's a rustling sound as she pulls out another cigarette. She puts it in her mouth but doesn't light it.

"No. He's the worst father ever. In fact, he's the worst person. He cheats, he lies, and when things don't go his way, he throws in the towel and walks out."

She tips her head to one side. "But there are worse fathers."

"Such as?"

"Well, please don't repeat this, Jay, because you could get me sent home." She slides closer to me along the bench. "I don't think that Mr. Briscoe is the world's best father."

I must be in a dark spot because she's only a couple of feet away from me and she hasn't said anything about my face.

"He seems okay to me."

"He's a nice enough guy. He's decent to me, but as a father he's something else." She takes the unlit cigarette from her mouth and twirls it around in her fingers. "He practically forces Malcolm to look at porn."

"Okay. That's a little weird I admit, but maybe it's just his thing." I have to look away. I can't look at Siggur while she's talking about porn. Not even her silhouette. I stare at the concrete floor.

"Don't you ever wonder why?"

It's a good question. I think I just thought it was a good idea, but maybe there is something behind it. "Maybe he wants Malcolm to be open about sex."

"He thinks Malcolm's gay." I bite my lip so I don't laugh. She goes quiet. I look up at her, and she's staring hard at me. I realize she must have wanted me to look straight at her so I wouldn't think she was bullshitting. "He thinks he can straighten him out by making him look at the right kind of porn."

I shrug. "Does that work?"

"No. Of course not! Silly." She leans back and looks at the ceiling.

"Is Malcolm gay?"

"I have no idea. Maybe he isn't anything yet, but *that* isn't the point. The point is that he's trying to turn Malcolm into something he isn't. Can you imagine how hard that is for Malcolm?" She spreads her hands as if she's holding a huge boulder, or maybe the millstone Malcolm has to carry.

"Yes. I mean, no. I can't imagine. It must be awful."

She leans close to me again. I can tell she's smiling by the way the side of her face bulges. "Then there's the business with you and Tinga."

"Oh, man." Now it's my turn to stare at the ceiling.

"It was you," she says. "Am I right?"

For one second I consider telling her I have no idea what she's talking about, but only for one second. From her tone of voice, I realize she's doing more than just making a wild guess.

"I suppose so," I say. Not much point in denying it now anyway.

"Nobody in the Briscoe household knew it was you, but I put two and two together. I was watching you and Tinga at the pool. I could tell there was something going on there." She keeps smiling, but looks at me from the corner of her eye. "Anyway, Tinga's new boyfriend has been a big topic of conversation in the Briscoe household. I don't know how true this is, but he was supposed to have stolen Tinga from Malcolm."

"That's not really true," I say, but as soon as the words are out of my mouth I realize that it probably is true.

"I don't know if it's completely untrue, Mr. Jay, but that's not the point." She looks serious again. "Do you know what? Malcolm told me he was actually glad to have Tinga out of his hair. But then his father went to work on him." She points out of the shelter in the direction of the Briscoes' house. "Mister Briscoe started following Malcolm around the house, taunting him. He even told Malcolm he'd seen some youth holding hands with Tinga"—she raises her eyebrows in fake shock—"and kissing her. And then he said, *A real man would not take this lying down.* By the end of the week, Malcolm was ready to kill someone."

I nod while I mull this over. I can't think of what to say. It all adds up. Malcolm is no psycho. His dad pushed him into it.

Another car passes and shadows from the poplar trees are thrown across us. My head feels a little clearer. I should make my way home and clean myself up. I stand and hitch up my shorts. Luckily the little problem I had earlier has gone. "I was just on my way back from the dojo. I went there to try to make things up with Tinga."

"You had a row?" Siggur stands up and moves in front of me as if to block my exit. I'm glad she doesn't want me to go.

"No. We split up. I actually dumped her."

"Jay, that's not good." She puts her hands on my shoulders.

"You're telling me." I can't look her in the eye, so I stare at the floor. There's just enough light that I can make out a used a condom. It makes me gag, so I look away again. "It was really stupid, and I did it for a stupid reason. I dumped her because I felt bad about stealing her from Malcolm. I felt that stealing someone else's girlfriend was the kind of thing my dad would do, and I won't do anything he does, so the only thing I could think of to do was to tell her to go back to Malcolm."

"Now you want her to give you another chance?"

"Do you think I stand a chance?"

"I don't know, Jay. Was Malcolm at the dojo?"

I laugh. "Oh yeah. Malcolm was there."

"Was everything okay with him when he saw you?"

I don't know what to say to this. "I should go or I'll be late." Then something occurs to me. "Are you heading back to the Briscoes? I'm heading that way."

"Nah. I don't have to be back till eight, so I'm going to have one more smoke first."

There's a couple of clicks, a spark, and then Siggur's lighter flares, filling the shelter with flickering orange light.

"Jay. For Christ's sake! Your face! What's happened?"

"I fell down some stairs."

"Did Malcolm do this?"

"I can't remember. I sparred with an eleven-year-old girl. I think it might have been her."

"Jay, we have to get you to a hospital."

"No. I'm just going to walk home. I'll be fine tomorrow."

"Jay, you're crazy. I'm going to call an ambulance."

"It's really okay."

"Please. Do this for me, just to be on the safe side. There's a phone booth just behind the shelter. Stay here. I'm going to call."

I sit back down on the bench, and I must have fallen asleep for a second, because it seems like she's only gone a couple of seconds. She unzips her Harrington jacket. "Here," she says. I try not to look at the bulges her breasts make in her T-shirt. Before I can move away, she slides the sleeves over my arms like she's dressing a little kid.

She's an au pair. This is something she knows how to do.

Before I can resist, she's fastened the zipper up to my neck. Now I'm the one who has to act like a child and throw it off, but I don't really want to. It's warm and it has her smell: flowery and smoky.

She rubs her shoulders and makes a burr with her lips.

"Aren't you going to be cold?"

"I'm dry, and I have a two-minute walk home."

Suddenly I'm afraid—or at least I'm almost afraid. I'm trying not to think about anything too much because my thoughts are lined up like a bunch of black belts I have to fight. Funny how you can be afraid of things that have already happened. "Are you going to leave me here?"

"No, silly boy. Look, don't fall asleep until you see the doctor." She sits down next to me and puts her arm around my shoulders. "If you're going to ask Tinga for a second chance, would you ever think about giving your dad a second chance?"

"I don't know if I can," I say, but as soon as I say it I realize that if I can stay awake, I can probably do just about anything.

A siren wails in the distance.

TWENTY-THREE

I wake up to find *Mother!* standing beside the sofa with a cup of tea.

So much for a concussion.

"Someone's here to see you," she says.

For half a second my heart leaps. Even though it would be utterly impossible in any configuration of events, I think it's going to be Tinga.

Absolutely every inch of my body hurts when I half-turn to see who it is.

I've only been awake for a minute and I'm already sick of the neck brace.

Then when I actually see who it is, I feel even worse.

"You look horrible," says Malcolm.

"You're too kind," I say. Even though it kills my neck, I look up at him. He has a decent shiner. The edge of his eye is swollen up into a yellow-and-blue hump.

"I didn't realize I did that to you," he says, and pulls a pained look.

"Um. You didn't. I fell down some stairs on the way home."

"Yeah. Sure," he says, like he doesn't believe me. "I suppose I don't look so fantastic myself."

"I'll trade with you," I say. He stands in the doorway looking around. "Sit here." I wave my hand towards where I think the armchair is, although obviously I can't turn my head to look at it. But he stays in the doorway, holding a brown paper bag like he might throw up into it.

"I'm sorry," I say for the umpteenth time in the last few hours. The difference is that this time I mean it. I'm not saying sorry because I'm scared of Malcolm beating me up. I don't suppose he'd come over here to do that. I don't have a third eye or a second nose for him to mess up, so he'll have to wait for a couple of weeks till the scabs come off and he can see where he's punching.

I really am sorry—it's just that I'm not completely sure what I'm apologizing to Malcolm for. I'm definitely apologizing for punching him, which was an accident, but I'm not apologizing for taking Tinga away from him, which I did on purpose.

It's a funny old world, but I'm not really up for self-analysis just at the moment.

"I got you something." He steps into the room and waves the paper bag in front of my face.

"Ah, man. You didn't have to do that." I pull the disk out of the bag. "*Police Story Two*, starring Jackie Chan," I read. "Thanks, mate." I reach out my free hand and we do the manly right-angle hand clasp.

"Want to watch it now?"

"Yeah. Why not? You mind putting it in the player?"

"No problem," he says. He opens the case and goes over to the machine. When he has his back to me, he says, "I didn't really mind about you and Tinga, you know."

"Uh huh," I say. This takes me a little by surprise, and being surprised without moving my head isn't as easy as it sounds.

"It wasn't my idea." He fiddles with something on the DVD player. I guess this is because he doesn't want to look at me.

I click it on and the FBI warning comes up.

Malcolm starts to say something with his back to me, which I'm pretty sure is the story Siggur already told me, so I say, "Look, let's watch the movie," over what he's starting to say. If I was going to take the trouble to put together a top-ten list of things I don't want to talk about, then I think Malcolm's dad would be near the top. "It's good to see you, mate. Thanks for coming."

It's a brilliant choice. Well, almost. Jackie Chan is every bit as brilliant as Bruce Lee, only Jackie Chan is funny as well. I manage to find a combination of pillows and cushions that can support my head, but I can't laugh. Who would have thought that laughing could be so painful?

After about half an hour, I can hardly keep my eyes open, plus I think it might be about time I get to take the codeine.

"Look, I don't want to be rude, but I'm not feeling very social right now. I need to get a little shut-eye."

"No. That's okay. I just wanted to check you were still alive," says Malcolm, and he stands up.

"What's your verdict?"

He ignores my question and says, "I have a little something else for you."

"Aw, c'mon. You got me Jackie Chan. You don't have to do this."

He moves the chair in front of him so it's between us.

"It's actually information. There's this church called Saint Ethelberger's on Elm Grove. It's a big red-brick thing, right on the corner. Anyway, Tinga goes to choir practice after school on Wednesday evenings. She gets out at five, then goes up to Churchill Square to get the bus home. I used to meet her there now and again. She's probably still doing it."

TWENTY-FOUR

I sort of had this idea that by the time Wednesday rolled around, I would be able to take off the neck brace, so I tried it.

Not a good idea.

When you're wearing a neck brace, everybody gives you a second look, and not because you remind them of their favorite soap-opera star, so by the time I get to Saint Ethelberger's I'm feeling pretty self-conscious.

But on the other hand, you look weird, so nobody questions any odd behavior.

At about five to five, kids in Cardinal Newman uniforms start to spill out of the front door in ones and twos. Quite a few of them produce cigarette packs. They light up with the kind of urgency that makes it look like they want to get the smell of incense out of their lungs as soon as they can.

The fearlike feeling floods through me about half a second before I see her. I'm not sure what I have left to be afraid of. Success maybe. She runs down the steps with her hands shoved in her jacket pockets. She stops a sparring distance away from me and folds her lips over her teeth, but then takes a step closer. She gives me the sort of smile that they probably train undertakers to give bereaved relatives.

I want to say, *Look, Tinga, I really want us to be together. Couldn't you just give me one more chance?* That's what I planned to say, but as I'm about to open my mouth, a Pakistani-looking girl comes up behind Tinga's left and taps her right shoulder.

Tinga does the two-way head turn.

The dark-haired girl looks pleased with herself. "Hey, Tinga. You walking up to Churchill Square?" She's quite a bit taller than Tinga. She's pretty with a longish nose.

"Yeah, I'll follow you up there, Denise," says Tinga.

When the girl's out of earshot, I say, "I decided to stop beating myself up and let somebody else have the fun."

She does her smile-frown-smile thing, only the opposite way around this time so she ends up frowning.

"Jay. It looks awful. I'm so sorry it happened. Does it hurt?"

"See ya, Ting!" A blonde girl slaps Tinga's shoulder and heads towards the seafront.

"Now and again," I say, which is true. I don't know what to do with my hands, and I realize it's because I want to hug her. I shove my hands into my pockets and say exactly what Hugh told me. "I wanted to invite you to something."

"I don't know, Jay." She points over my shoulder. "I have to get the bus. Do you want to walk a bit?"

"Sure. My legs still work okay." I grin at her. "It's just everything else that doesn't."

She doesn't smile back though. Not even a smile-frown. Not even an undertaker's smile.

"Don't get me wrong," she says. "I really like you, but it's not easy. I have to ration my lies, and Denise can only account for so much. I'm not like you. I can't just walk out of the front door."

It's not a *no*. But isn't quite a *yes*.

"I guarantee that you'll really like it," I say.

"Can't you tell me what it is?"

"I wanted it to be a surprise."

"You want me to agree to come to something with you even though I don't know what it is?"

"Yeah. That's exactly what I want." This is Hugh's plan, and it's starting to look a bit hollow.

When we reach Western Road, she runs ahead of me to the curb and looks left.

I catch up.

"It's my bus." She brushes her hair out of her face. "The nineteen. I have to get this one. Sorry."

"I wish you could stay longer."

"Me too." She strokes the back of my hand. I turn my hand over and take hold of hers. She squeezes my fingers and then lets go.

Somehow that tiny gesture sends a wave of sadness right over me.

"Typical," she says, and raises her eyebrows. "They always come in threes for some reason."

I follow her eyes to where the bus is stuck in a traffic jam at the top of North Road. I can just see the two other buses behind. All of them are nineteens.

"So." She has her back to me. I move closer to her. The bus stop's crowded and I don't want anyone else to hear what I have to say. Her hair whips into my face. "Can you come tomorrow?"

She ignores my question and says, "I know it sounds corny, Jay, but from the moment I saw you I had the biggest crush on you." She turns around to face me and takes hold of both my wrists.

"I mean, the moment I saw you from a distance." She looks back over her shoulder at the buses, but they haven't moved. "I saw you through the window at the newsagent's. When you actually came over and stood next to me, my knees went weak. I had to hold on to the magazine rack to stop myself from falling over."

She strokes my cheek, then licks her lips.

"I would have gone off with you right there and then. I could tell that you didn't have a clue what to do about me, and that made you even nicer. You didn't have all the right things to say. I hate it when blokes try to charm me. They say nice things they don't mean, but they say them because they want something. Like they're trying to sell me shoes. So, you see, I liked you before I knew anything about who you are, or what your dad does, or what you were like apart from what I could tell from looking at you."

"But you only seemed to get interested in me when you found out my dad was in films," I say.

"Jay! I got interested because I had something I could talk to you about. I didn't know what to say before that. I was tongue-tied. As soon as you mentioned films, I thought, *Brilliant.* Finally I can speak to him and he won't think I'm a total moron."

This makes me laugh even though I can't think of a time I've been more unhappy. Even though she's telling me really nice things, I know it's all over. Granny Smallfield was probably right about first girlfriends. They probably never do work out. Even if she's right about there being many more, I still don't want this one to end before it's even started.

She glances back at the buses. The front one is moving forward, although slowly.

"Don't get me wrong." She buttons up her jacket as if it's just gotten cold. "I'm not saying that you're film-star good-looking, because you aren't. But you're not bad. Not bad at all."

"What? Not even with this on?" I tap the neck brace.

There's a rush of air and we're thrown into a chilly shadow as the bus pulls up. The crowd jostles itself into a queue. Tinga grasps my wrist and pulls me with her as she gets into line.

"Tinga," I say into her ear, "will you come with me to this thing tomorrow? I have to know. I have to set it up."

"Jay. I'm sorry. I can't do it."

"But why?" An icy wave of grief breaks over my head. For the first time since I was a little kid, I actually want to weep.

"It's too long to explain and I have to go home."

"Are you in the queue?" says a woman behind me. She

has a baby cradled in one arm and a folded up buggy in the other.

"No." I take a step off to the side, in between the bus and the queue, and watch Tinga step up through the door.

Is that it?

That's the end?

I watch Tinga show her pass, then climb up to the top deck.

"You getting on or what, Sunshine?"

I turn around and look straight into the red face of an old codger behind me. At first I just think this is his sarcy way of telling me to get out the way, and I'm in the mood to give him some lip.

"Come on, Tosh." Now it's the bus driver. "What are you waiting for? Christmas? Get on, or get out of the bloody way."

Then this mumbling starts behind me. "What are you, thirteen? Fourteen? Probably think there's nothing worse in the world than being thirteen, but I'll tell you what's worse. Being seventy." I wheel around. It's the old codger. "If you let 'em go as easily as that, you're never going to be able to hold on to 'em."

She had a crush on me? Her knees went weak? "Yeah," I say, and jump up onto the deck.

The driver yells, "That's enough. We're full."

The automatic doors hiss shut behind me.

Through the glass, the red-faced bloke looks like he wished he'd strangled me when he had the chance, which would have been tricky with the neck brace.

Did he really say what I thought he said? Or did I just imagine it? I'm not sure which would be weirder.

I shake the idea out of my head and show the driver my pass.

"No seats upstairs," he says, as if he's been watching the whole scene between me and Tinga. "Standing only. Downstairs."

I'm thrown towards the back as the bus jerks forward. I cling to the rails and make my way towards the stairs. I glance at the driver, but he's concentrating on the traffic.

I swing around and clamber to the upper deck.

Tinga is two-thirds of the way down. She's looking out of the window and doesn't see me.

The seats are all full, just as the driver said. I didn't really think this through. I won't be able to talk to Tinga because I can't sit next to her, and she hasn't even seen me because she's totally preoccupied with what's going on out of the window. Then it hits me. She's twisted around, looking back towards Churchill Square. Is she hoping for one last look at me?

I hold on tight to the metal safety bar like I'm on a ship in a storm. The brakes squeal. The bus is slowing for the next stop. There's no point in this. I should get off. I turn to go down the steps when I notice someone behind me from the corner of my eye.

A couple gets up from the same seat. They give me a not-quite-sympathetic look as they shove past me towards the stairs.

"Go ahead," I say, but their looks don't say, *We're sorry*

you're hurt, and somebody should give you a seat. They say, *We're sorry you're too stupid to realize there isn't a seat for you.*

The empty seat is across from Tinga.

Holding on to the rail, I make a dash for the seat. I swing from the metal poles like a monkey. Meanwhile, the bloke who was squashed into the middle of the back seat stands up and tries to get there first.

We're about the same distance. I speed up, and so does he, but in a flurry of movement someone else gets there first.

Tinga.

She slides across to the window, gives me her smile-frown-smile, and pats the seat next to her.

I flop into the seat. Her smile freezes and fades. She turns away from me as if there's something interesting in the shops we're passing.

Without looking at me she says, "You know that Friday when you came to the park? I saw you. You went into the café. I followed you and looked through the window, and you were chatting to Siggur. I thought you were going out with her. I was beside myself."

I didn't know that, but I have no idea what to say. I wish I'd known.

She turns and faces me. "Then you came out, and Colin pulled you off your bike, and if he hadn't run away I would have thumped him. Probably would have been suicidal, but I would have done it for you. I was so worried about you, because you seemed so lost. But the problem, Jay, is that I'm worried for me."

My hand is on the seat between us. She slides her hand

over my knuckles and folds her fingers between mine. Am I still in the running?

"You're so wrapped up in yourself and the strange things you imagine. You don't really give a lot of thought to anyone else. You think I'm some kind of Barbie doll you can take out of her box when you want to play, but I'm not. My life goes on when you don't see me. You don't know anything about me."

She picks up my hand and clasps it between both of hers.

"You don't know about my parents, or if they're together. You don't know about school. You don't even know if I have any brothers or sisters. Jay, I hate saying these things to you, because I don't want to hurt you and I think you're a very easy person to hurt."

I draw my hand out from her grasp, place my arm across her shoulder, and pull her towards me. "I can change. I can be different," I say.

At first she tenses up. "I just don't know," she says, and then very slowly—almost too slow to notice—she shuffles towards me under my arm. It's not like we're back together and I can kiss her, but it's better than it was. She holds onto the hand that's over her shoulder and says, "I have to think about myself. I hurt easily, too. Did you know that?"

"But you'll come with me tomorrow?"

"Seems like I don't have a choice."

TWENTY-FIVE

So I actually take Tinga to see Dad. I know it sounds daft but, well, it worked for Malcolm. He took her to meet his parents. I'm going one better though.

We meet Dad at the Cricketers, a pub near the seafront.

"There he is. That's him in the khaki." I pull Tinga's arm as if she can't see him, but she can see him every bit as well as I can on the other side of the glass.

There's an ear-splitting crash as he comes through the big plate-glass window holding onto a blond-haired bloke. They both roll across the pavement, shards flying everywhere. The blond bloke gets up first and goes to kick my dad in the face while he's still on his knees, but my dad grabs his foot and flips him over. Then my dad tries to grab the bloke while he's on his back, but the bloke sticks his foot in my dad's stomach and flips him onto his back.

The blond bloke picks up a two-by-four from the broken window frame and hits my dad with it until the two-by-four breaks. The bloke kicks my dad in the face a couple of times, then legs it towards the beach.

My dad just lies there curled up in a heap.

"What do we do?" whispers Tinga into my ear.

"Cut!" yells a woman.

"It's a wrap!" shouts someone else. "Lunch!"

Immediately the street is crowded with PAs, grips, and electricians.

My dad gets to his feet. He looks like he's gained about ten stone. He brushes the broken glass off his uniform as a woman picks up the pieces of the window frame.

The blond bloke reappears and punches my dad on the arm. "Good one, Trev."

"Yeah." My dad grins at the blond bloke and says, "See you later, Martin."

Dad catches sight of me and waves. He comes over, pulling big strips of Styrofoam out of his uniform, which starts to hang off him like it's five sizes too big.

"Jason of the Argonauts," he says. He reaches out and squeezes my shoulder. He looks shorter. A lot shorter than the last time. He points to my neck brace. "I see you're wearing the family uniform."

I think about saying something very rude, but I'm on my best behavior. "This is Tinga." I reach out and let my hand hover an inch or two above her shoulder, but no lower. I'm not sure I'm allowed to touch her.

My dad breaks into a broad grin when he looks at her.

His special smile for pretty females. "So. You're Jason's girl-friend?"

I squeeze my eyes shut and look away. How can he say exactly the wrong thing the first time he opens his mouth?

"Yup," says Tinga.

What!

I turn to face her. Does she mean this?

Or is she just telling a white lie to keep things simple? I try to catch her eye but her attention seems to be on my dad, who's removing some kind of padding from inside his jacket. He puts the padding under his arm, looks at me and then back to Tinga, and says, "Why?"

Tinga reddens. I hadn't realized before, but that's my dad's special talent. Not being thrown out of windows, not being blown up, not being bitten in half, but embarrassing people.

Now Tinga looks at me. She says, "He's kind. He's brainy." She looks at my dad and shrugs. "He's cute."

"Funny how fashions change," says my dad, still flash-ing his teeth at Tinga.

Maybe I should keep up with the karate. After all, there will have to come a time when I can punch him in the nose. Maybe he never learned any manners because he never needed them.

"What's the story?" I say, instead of kicking him in the shins.

"It's pretty good actually," says Dad. "It's called *Where There's Smoke*. It's a war-time drama, set in a seaside town." He claps his hands together. "It's actually about deserters from the British Armed Forces. A lot of them ended up hiding out in resort towns along the coast." He grins at Tinga again. "That stunt was for Timothy Spall. He's part of the military police tracking them down." He points to his MP armband.

"So you're actually a cop this time," I say. "One of the good guys."

"Weeeeell." He scratches his big square chin. "It's not so clear cut. The MPs are on the side of the law, but they're still capturing the unwilling and shipping them off for a spell in the brig, followed by being sent to the heat of the action." He pulls a sad face. "Which is pretty nasty."

"But you're more good than bad, then?" I say.

He scratches his chin again. "About sixty-forty." He nods at me, which gives me an odd sensation. I can't remember a time when he's ever agreed with me.

"So that's an improvement on a storm trooper or a zombie or"—I can't resist this—"a demented chimpanzee."

"No. No sixty-forty for storm troopers or zombies." He laughs, then he grins at me. It's not quite the full-on fog-lamp grin he's been giving Tinga, but it's better than any smile he's ever given me before. "They are bad through and through. I don't know about demented chimpanzees though. I feel sorry for them."

Martin, my dad's blond antagonist, comes up and slaps Dad on the back. "Come on, Trev," he says. My dad stumbles forward and makes a choking sound as if Martin's slap has actually hurt him, then he swivels and punches Martin in the gut. Martin folds up and retches, but even I can see that my dad's fist didn't make contact.

Then Martin straightens up and says, "Duty calls."

I study cloud formations and seagulls, and imagine I'm far away. Tinga laughs, though, which I'm guessing is the whole point of the exercise.

I like hearing Tinga laugh. Malcolm makes her laugh, and even my dad makes her laugh, but I seem to have lost the knack. Maybe I could learn something from the old man after all.

"Well, it's very nice to meet you." I look back down to earth and of course my father is speaking to Tinga, not me. He puts out a hand and Tinga puts hers in it.

"Nice meeting you, too," she says. "Can I ask you something?"

"Fire away."

"Does it hurt. All that being punched and kicked and stuff?"

"Not right away, but I feel it the next day, and for a while afterwards, but then as soon as I get paid I seem to make a miraculous recovery." He turns to me and the smile vanishes. "So you're going to come back. Right?"

"Right," I repeat, which doesn't really commit me to anything.

After my dad leaves, I buy Tinga coffee. I want to talk to her, but the café is too crowded. I don't want anyone listening to what I have to say, so I wait till I walk her back to the bus stop.

I look at her ear for a while, then she turns to face me.

Maybe this isn't a time for words. I twist at my waist, which isn't very comfortable, and plant a kiss right on her mouth.

She doesn't scream for the police, she doesn't shout *kee-yah!* and deck me with a flurry of punches and kicks. She just asks, "Why do you want to be with me?"

"I don't know," I say, and laugh. "Because you're you. I really like you. And you're also very cute."

"You need these," she says. She takes off her glasses, flips them over, and pushes then onto my face. She turns into a blob. I can just make out the two brown blobs of her eyes, and the red blob of her mouth. The red blob comes towards me and I feel something soft and warm pressed against my mouth.

About the Author

Ed Briant took up martial arts because he liked swimming.

Ed was born by the ocean in the city of Brighton, England. At that time, Brighton beach was famous as a battleground for rival gangs of mods, punks, skinheads, and bikers. Ed liked swimming in the ocean, but in order to get from the city to the ocean it was necessary to pass through the fighting gangs. With this in mind, Ed spent many years studying Karate, Tae Kwon Do, and Boxing so he could defend himself *en route*.

As it turned out, by the time Ed was proficient at the choppy-socky arts, the mods had started to wear last year's fashions, the punks had jobs, the skinheads had grown their hair, and the bikers were driving station wagons. In short, nobody cared much for fighting anymore.

Ed can now reach the ocean in perfect safety in his current home of Savannah, Georgia, at which point all he needs to worry about are cramps, bull sharks, and rip tides. Ed has two daughters, teaches illustration, and occasionally practices roundhouse kicks in the kitchen when he thinks nobody's watching.